W9-BMF-111

THE FABLED
FOURTH
GRADERS
OF
AESOP
ELEMENTARY
SCHOOL

THE FABLED FOURTH GRADERS OF AESOP ELEMENTARY SCHOOL

Candace Fleming

SCHOLASTIC INC.
New York Toronto London Auckland Sydney
Mexico City New Delhi Hong Kong Buenos Aires

For Eric, who listened, laughed, and dispensed loads of bad puns. What would I do without you?

This is a work of fiction. Names, characters, places, and incidents either are the product of the author's imagination or are used fictitiously. Any resemblance to actual persons, living or dead, events, or locales is entirely coincidental.

No part of this publication may be reproduced, stored in a retrieval system, or transmitted in any form or by any means, electronic, mechanical, photocopying, recording, or otherwise, without written permission of the publisher. For information regarding permission, write to Schwartz & Wade Books, an imprint of Random House Children's Books, a division of Random House, Inc., 1745 Broadway, New York, NY 10019.

ISBN-13: 978-0-545-19813-4
ISBN-10: 0-545-19813-5

Copyright © 2007 by Candace Fleming. All rights reserved. Published by Scholastic Inc., 557 Broadway, New York, NY 10012, by arrangement with Schwartz & Wade Books, an imprint of Random House Children's Books, a division of Random House, Inc. SCHOLASTIC and associated logos are trademarks and/or registered trademarks of Scholastic Inc.

12 11 10 9 8 7 6 5 4 3 2 1   9 10 11 12 13 14/0

Printed in the U.S.A.   40

First Scholastic printing, September 2009

The text of this book is set in Nimrod and Congress Sans.
Book design by Rachael Cole

CONTENTS

The Principal Struggles   1

Mr. Jupiter Goes Fourth   6

An Absentminded Morning   13

The Librarian in Love   18

Picture Day   22

Dance, Stanford, Dance   31

Calvin Goes to Kindergarten   43

The Boy Who Cried Lunch Monitor   57

Please Don't Tease Ashley Z.   67

Pffft!   77

There Once Was a Man from Dancart . . .   84

The Bad, the Beautiful, and the Stinky   98

Dewey or Don't We?   106

Ham and Beans   121

Missy's Lost Mittens   130

Sticks and Stones   138

March Madness   142

Catch!   144

The Problem with Being Ernest   153

Humphrey's Lunch   163

The Spelling Goddess   168

First Kiss   172

Mr. Jupiter Takes the Fifth   176

THE PRINCIPAL STRUGGLES

THE SOON-TO-BE FOURTH GRADERS AT
Aesop Elementary School had a reputation for being—

"Precocious," said their former first-grade teacher, Ms. Bucky. She ground her teeth.

"High-energy," added their second-grade teacher, Mrs. Chen. The muscle beneath her jaw twitched.

"Robust," agreed their third-grade teacher, Mr. Frost. He patted his now all-white hair.

"Humph!" snorted Bertha Bunz, the lunchroom monitor. "Those kids are just plain naughty." Because she wasn't a teacher, Mrs. Bunz felt free to speak the truth.

Mrs. Bunz was right. So *special* were the incoming fourth graders that no teacher dared set foot in what would soon be their classroom.

"Not for love or money," shivered Ms. Bucky.

"Not for all the tea in China," shuddered Mrs. Chen.

"Ye gods, no!" yelped Mr. Frost.

It was the last day of summer vacation, and Mrs. Struggles, Aesop Elementary's principal, was at her wits' end. "School starts tomorrow, and I still don't have a fourth-grade teacher," she moaned. "What am I going to do?"

"Have you placed a want ad?" suggested Ms. Bucky.

"Spoken with the superintendent?" suggested Mrs. Chen.

"Talked with the school board?" suggested Mr. Frost.

"Humph!" Mrs. Bunz snorted again. "Call a zookeeper!"

Mrs. Struggles ignored the remark. Defeated, she shuffled into her office and flopped into her chair. *If Aesop Elementary were bigger,* she thought, *I would have separated the troublemakers long ago.* But the school was small—only one classroom per grade level—so the kids had to stay together. Rubbing her throbbing temples, she sighed, "How I wish a teacher would walk through that door."

At that precise moment, a breeze blew through the principal's office. It rustled the papers on her desk, rattled her window blinds, and flung open the door to

2

reveal a tall, dark man wearing a pith helmet and clutching a copy of the morning's want ads.

"I am Mr. Jupiter," he said. "I have come about the teaching job."

Mrs. Struggles rubbed her eyes. Was this a dream? she wondered.

But no, Mr. Jupiter was still there.

"You *are* looking for a fourth-grader teacher, aren't you?" he asked.

Mrs. Struggles nodded, her spirits suddenly soaring. Waving Mr. Jupiter into a seat, she said, "Tell me a bit about yourself."

"Where to begin?" he replied. "My first job was as an assistant dog groomer aboard King Bernard's yacht, the SS *Pooch,* anchored off the Dalmatian coast. After receiving my degree in nanothermal economics from Dummer University, I led an expedition in search of the dodo bird. Later, I conducted the Timbuktu Philharmonic Orchestra, worked as a translator for Bigfoot, became the first man to ski down Mount Everest, collected mummified cats in Egypt, and discovered the lost city of Atlantis." He smiled. "Among other things."

Mrs. Struggles tapped her desk with a pencil. He certainly sounded interesting.

"Do you have any teaching experience?" she asked.

"Some," replied Mr. Jupiter. "I was head tetherball coach at Matilda Jane's School for Prim and Proper Girls in Las Vegas, as well as the swimming instructor at Loch Ness Middle School. I also taught Swahili as a second language at Dooglehorn Elementary in Switzerland, hula dancing at Balderdash Academy for Boys in London, and organic geochemistry at Harvard." He smiled again. "Among other places."

Mrs. Struggles tapped her desk some more. He sounded experienced, but . . .

"Have you worked with high-energy students?"

"I studied for a year at the Coochie-Coochie Institute for Misbehaved Monkeys," said Mr. Jupiter. He smiled a third time. "Among other schools."

Mrs. Struggles kept tapping.

"Is there anything else you'd like to add?" she finally asked.

Mr. Jupiter shook his head. "Nothing important," he said, "although you might be interested to know I attended fifth grade at this very school."

Mrs. Struggles stopped tapping. "You did?" she exclaimed. "Really? Who was your teacher?"

Her question caused Mr. Jupiter to turn as white as his whale tooth necklace.

But Mrs. Struggles didn't notice. Leaping to her feet, she cried, "Why didn't you tell me this earlier?" She extended her hand. "You're hired! Welcome back to Aesop Elementary, Mr. Jupiter."

MR. JUPITER GOES FOURTH

ON THE FIRST DAY OF SCHOOL, MR. Jupiter wrote his name on the blackboard.

"Welcome to fourth grade," he said to his nineteen new students. "I am your teacher, Mr. Jupiter."

"Jupiter?" repeated Humphrey Parrot. "Jupiter? That's a funny name."

"It's not as funny as Pluto," said Bruce Vanderbanter.

"Or Uranus," added Lenny Wittier.

The boys high-fived. "Mr. Uranus! Mr. Uranus! Mr. Uranus!"

They glanced at the new teacher, waiting for a reaction.

But Mr. Jupiter just smiled. "I'm glad to know my students have a sense of humor," he said.

Then—

POP!

In the back of the room, Bernadette Braggadoccio peeled a glob of pink bubble gum off her nose and shoved it back into her mouth. She chomped, smacked, and pulled long, sticky strings from her mouth. Then she huffed . . . and puffed . . . and peered over the top of her bubble at the new teacher.

She waited for a reaction.

But Mr. Jupiter was still smiling. "Chewing gum is known to help children concentrate," he said.

Then—

> *"Down by the banks of the Hanky Panky,*
> *Where the bullfrogs hop from banky to banky,*
> *The momma frogs get so cranky cranky*
> *That they give their tadpoles a spanky spanky."*

On the other side of the room, Missy Place and Rose Clutterdorf SMACK-SLAP-CLAPPED their hands to the rhythm of their words.

But their eyes were on the new teacher, waiting for a reaction.

Mr. Jupiter was still smiling. "What a wonderful exercise for improving eye-hand coordination," he said.

Then—

"I know a poem," shouted Lillian Ditty—Lil, for short. "Want to hear it?" And she waxed poetic:

"Oh, homework! Oh, homework!
Here's the true scoop.
It takes so much time
That I can't even—"

"Poop!" hollered Hamilton Samitch—Ham to his friends. "Did you know that the dung beetle rolls, buries, and eats poop? Isn't that fascinating? Dung beetles are my newest hobby. I'd rather study them than—"

"Play ball!" shrieked Jackie Jumpbaugh.

She tossed a crumpled piece of paper to Calvin Tallywong, who lobbed it to Amisha Spelwadi, who bumped it to Emberly Everclass, who juggled it onto Rachel Piffle's desk.

"Pffft," mumbled Rachel. She blushed and swept the paper into the trash can.

"Two points!" shrieked Jackie.

"Rah!" cheered Ashlee Anderson.

"Rah!" cheered Ashleigh Brown.

"Shish-boom-blaahh-blaahh-blaahh," mocked Ashley Zamboni.

"What's the matter?" teased Lenny. "Don't you want to cheer like the other girls?"

"I'm a boy!" hollered Ashley Z. "And don't you forget it!"

Behind them, Victoria Sovaine smirked. "You guys are sooooo obnoxious." She tossed a golden curl over her shoulder and glanced at the new teacher.

The entire class waited for a reaction.

Incredibly, Mr. Jupiter was still smiling. "You are a unique group of children," he remarked.

At that moment, Mrs. Struggles knocked on the classroom door. "May I speak with you for a moment?" she said to the new teacher.

Mr. Jupiter followed her into the hall.

Left alone, the fourth graders looked at one another.

"What's with this guy?" Emberly finally said. "He doesn't get upset about anything."

"Yeah, he doesn't get upset about anything," repeated Humphrey.

Bernadette folded a fresh piece of gum into her mouth. "I think it's time we took the *direct* approach."

The others let her words sink in.

The *direct* approach?

Everyone knew what could happen if they took the *direct* approach.

Last year, in third grade, Victoria had talked *directly* back to Mr. Frost. She had spent thirty minutes in Mrs. Struggles' office.

The year before, in second grade, Bruce had drawn a naughty picture of Mrs. Chen and pinned it *directly* onto the back of her blouse. He had spent an hour in Mrs. Struggles' office.

And the year before that, in first grade, Ham had *directly* bit Ms. Bucky on the foot after she refused to give him a second cheese stick. He had spent the next four Fridays talking with Mr. Sigmund, the school counselor.

Was rattling the new teacher worth that kind of risk?

"We have to let him know who's boss," urged Bernadette. "Otherwise he'll try to control things all year."

"So what do we do?" asked Rose.

"We could put a tack on his chair," suggested Calvin.

"Good thinking," said Bernadette. "Anyone else?"

"We could pelt him with spitballs," said Jackie.

"Great," said Bernadette. "Other ideas?"

"We could tie his shoelaces together," said Melvin Moody.

As usual, everyone ignored him.

"I know," said Humphrey. "We could loosen all the screws in his chair. When he sits down—"

"Mr. Jupiter lands on his moon!" howled Lenny.

"I love it," said Victoria.

"It's brilliant," said Missy.

"Moooooon!" laughed Melvin.

The others ignored him.

Then Stanford Binet—who had been silent the whole time—spoke up. "Get serious," he sniffed. "Which of you is brave enough to put that tack on his chair?"

Ashley Z. looked at Missy.

Missy looked at Bernadette.

Bernadette looked at Victoria.

"Oh, no," she said. "I spent way too much time in Mrs. Struggles' office last year."

"And who," Stanford went on, "is bold enough to pelt him with spitballs?"

Victoria looked at Melvin.

Melvin looked at Rachel.

Rachel looked at Bruce.

"No way," he said. "I learned my lesson."

"And who," Stanford continued, "knows how to un-bolt a chair?"

Jackie looked at Calvin.

Calvin looked at Amisha.

Amisha looked at Ham.

"Forget it," he said. "I'm cured."

At that moment, Mr. Jupiter stepped back into the room. He clapped his hands. "Enough with the introductions," he said briskly. "It's time we got to work. Everyone, please take out a piece of paper. We are going to take a pop quiz on the Italian Renaissance."

The children groaned.

"And Bernadette," the new teacher added, "spit out that gum."

MORAL: It is one thing to talk about it, another to do it.

AN ABSENTMINDED MORNING

ON THE SECOND DAY OF SCHOOL, MR.
Jupiter took attendance.

"Raise your hand if you're not here," he said.

The children looked at one another.

Then Jackie's hand shot into the air. "I'm not here," she snickered. "I've gone to the national tetherball tournament to see the Hoboken Blowfish take on the Altoona Poodles."

The other students giggled, but Mr. Jupiter calmly said, "A reasonable excuse." He wrote Jackie's name on the attendance slip. Then he asked, "Is anyone else absent?"

"Me," said Bruce. "I'm staying home to play Meteor Monsters."

"Yeah," added Lenny, "and I'm staying with him. After all, the two-player version is the best."

"Perfectly understandable," said Mr. Jupiter. He wrote their names down too.

"I couldn't come to school today either," said Victoria. "I'm having a facial."

"I see," said Mr. Jupiter.

"And I couldn't come because I'm watching cartoons," said Emberly.

"Of course," said Mr. Jupiter.

"And I couldn't come because I ate too many hot dogs and got a stomachache," said Ham.

"My sympathies," said Mr. Jupiter.

Melvin waved his hand in the air. "Ask *me* why *I'm* not here!" he cried.

The others ignored him.

"Ask *me!*" cried Calvin.

"Why aren't you here?" asked Mr. Jupiter.

"Because I don't like school," replied Calvin.

"Hey," hollered Lenny, "that's why *I'm* not here."

"Get serious," snorted Stanford. "You already said you were playing video games with Bruce."

"For your information, Mr. Know-It-All-Smarty-Pants, I'm absent because I'm playing video games with Bruce *and* because I don't like school."

"That's too bad," said Mr. Jupiter. He wrote all their names on his attendance slip. "Is anyone else absent?"

"We are!" cried Ashlee A. and Ashleigh B.

"And me," added Ashley Z.

"And me," repeated Humphrey.

Mr. Jupiter took down their names. Then he pointed at Rose. "Are you here?"

"No," answered Rose. "I overslept."

"What about you?" Mr. Jupiter asked Missy.

Missy shook her head. "I got lost on the way to school."

"And you?" Mr. Jupiter looked at Rachel.

"Pffft," said Rachel.

"Beg your pardon?" said Mr. Jupiter.

"Pffft," Rachel said again.

"I'm sorry," said Mr. Jupiter. "What?"

"Pffft," said Rachel. "Pffft."

Mr. Jupiter shrugged and added her name to the slip.

"I'm not here either," Bernadette said with a dramatic sigh. "I just wasn't in the mood."

"Hey!" cried Lenny. "That's why *I'm* not here— because I wasn't in the mood, *and* I don't like school, *and* I'm playing video games with Bruce."

Stanford snorted. "Get serious."

Lenny smirked. "Get lost."

And Amisha raised her hand. "Don't forget about me," she said. "I'm not here either."

"Why not?" asked Mr. Jupiter.

Amisha thought a moment. "I'm visiting my grandparents in Calcutta," she finally said.

"Beautiful city," remarked Mr. Jupiter. "I once worked as an elephant trainer there."

Amisha smiled as Lil burst into verse:

"I'm writing a poem,
So I can't come to school.
I hope you'll forgive me
For being so cruel."

"Of course I will," said Mr. Jupiter. He wrote the last of the names on his attendance slip. Then he looked around the classroom. "Isn't anyone here today?"

Lenny shook his head. "It looks like you're all by yourself."

"Actually," said Mr. Jupiter, "I'm not here either."

"You're not?" said Bernadette.

"No," said Mr. Jupiter. "I'm trekking through the Amazon rain forest in search of the rare and elusive golden-throated rat-squirrel."

"You are?" said Amisha.

"I am," said Mr. Jupiter. "But don't worry. I have a substitute."

He plopped a human skull onto his desk.

The children stared, wide-eyed.

"This is Mrs. Yorick," Mr. Jupiter explained. "I found her on an archaeological dig along the Solo River in Java."

The children kept staring.

"Mrs. Yorick," continued Mr. Jupiter, "is never absent. Can you guess why?"

The children shook their heads.

"Because," he said, "she doesn't have any *body* to go out with."

For one moment, the children sat in silence.

Then Calvin chuckled.

Victoria giggled.

Soon all the children were rocking with laughter.

"No body," howled Lenny. "That's a good one, Mr. Jupiter."

"Thank you, Leonard," said Mr. Jupiter. "I thought it was pretty funny myself." And he laughed until his sides ached and his eyes teared.

Then they all got down to work.

MORAL: He laughs best who laughs last.

THE LIBRARIAN IN LOVE

MISS PAIGE TURNER, THE SCHOOL librarian, was busily cataloging new materials and reshelving books. Already she had hung her favorite poster on the wall behind the circulation desk. It read:

THERE IS A PLACE FOR EVERY BOOK,

AND EVERY BOOK HAS ITS PLACE.

Miss Turner considered this her motto. She loved nothing better than arranging her books neatly and numerically on the library shelves.

"Ah, the Dewey decimal system," she gushed as she stood back to admire her handiwork. "Humankind's single greatest achievement."

Then she turned to other tasks, her sensible brown loafers making a satisfying *shush-shush* sound as she bustled around the library. An hour earlier, the place had been crawling with students looking for *The Cat in the Hat, Ramona the Pest,* and books about dinosaurs. But now the library was quiet as a museum again— just the way Miss Turner liked it.

Then Mrs. Struggles walked in.

"Paige," she said, "I'd like you to meet Mr. Jupiter."

Annoyed at having her silence disturbed, Miss Turner frowned and looked up from the magazine rack she'd been arranging. She found herself looking into—

—the most beautiful pair of brown eyes in the whole world!

Instinctively, Miss Turner straightened her cardigan— the one with the apples appliquéd onto its pockets. She tucked back a strand of mouse-brown hair and pushed up her wire-rimmed glasses.

Mr. Jupiter smiled a dazzling smile. "Good afternoon," he said.

"Mr. Jupiter's our new fourth-grade teacher," explained Mrs. Struggles.

Miss Turner managed a weak "Hello." She felt like a scoop of vanilla ice cream on a hot summer's day— all sweet and drippy.

Mr. Jupiter leaned closer. "I look forward to working with you," he said. His voice caressed Miss Turner's pale skin like a soft spring breeze.

"Oh, me too," she breathed.

Mr. Jupiter leaned even closer. He was so close, the librarian could see the gold flecks in his eyes. "One more thing," he said.

"Anything," sighed Miss Turner.

"I would like to check out a copy of *Aesop's Fables*," he said. "Do I need to fill out a card?"

"What?" Miss Turner blinked. She felt blinded by his beauty. "No, no, take a copy, that's fine."

Mrs. Struggles raised her eyebrows. Miss Turner was always such a stickler for proper checkout procedures. What was going on here?

"Thank you," said Mr. Jupiter. He touched the back of her hand. "And when, may I ask, is it due?"

His touch jolted her senses. She felt confused. Dizzy. Electrified.

"Due?" she managed to croak. "Whenever."

Mrs. Struggles shook her head in disbelief. Miss Turner detested overdue books. Why, any student who didn't return a book within fourteen days was hunted down and fined.

Mr. Jupiter smiled again. "That is very generous of you, Paige. May I call you Paige?"

The sound of her name on his lips made her shiver.

"Of course."

"Mr. Jupiter," said Mrs. Struggles, "let me introduce you to our music teacher." She led him out the door.

Miss Turner stood there for a moment, dazed. Then

she collapsed into her swivel chair. It rolled across the floor and crashed into a shelving cart.

She barely noticed. Her heart raced, and a feeling of wild abandonment shot through her. Suddenly, she longed to kayak down the Congo River! Parachute off the Empire State Building! Read a trashy romance novel! With trembling hands, the librarian reached into her SO MANY BOOKS, SO LITTLE TIME book bag and pawed around until she found her compact. Snapping it open, she gazed at her reflection in the tiny mirror.

Just as she suspected, nothing had changed. And yet . . . Miss Turner shook her head. How odd! On the outside she looked exactly the same. But on the inside?

She felt like a brand-new woman.

MORAL: You can't judge a book by its cover.

PICTURE DAY

ROSE CLUTTERDORF HAD OVERSLEPT . . . again.

"Hurry! Hurry!" her mother cried.

Rose snatched yesterday's clothes off the floor and flung them on. She raced downstairs and—grabbing her backpack and a cold Toaster Tart—raced out the door. She didn't even take time to brush her teeth, or pee, or run a comb through her tangled hair.

Minutes later, she screeched into the classroom and—

Rose shook her head.

Why did everyone look so weird?

Ashlee A. was wearing a ruffled skirt and panty hose.

Ashleigh B. was wearing a shimmery green party dress.

And Ashley Z. was wearing dress pants and a collared shirt—and his shirt was tucked in!

The truth hit Rose like a ton of social studies books.

"Oh, no!" she gasped. "It's Picture Day!"

Victoria walked over to Rose and smirked. "You obviously forgot."

Victoria had dressed for Picture Day as if it were her wedding day. Her long blond hair had been swept up into a swirling mass of curls and hairpins. She was wearing a white velvet dress, white lace tights, and—

"Nice pearl collar," snickered Lenny.

"It looks like something my grandmother would wear," added Bruce.

"Or my basset hound," put in Emberly.

"Humph," snorted Victoria. "Boys don't know anything about fashion." And she flounced away.

Any other day, Rose wouldn't have cared what Victoria thought. She wouldn't have worried about her clothes or her hair. But today was different. Today was Picture Day.

Rose looked down at her wrinkled pink jeans and rumpled yellow T-shirt, which read MY GRANDMOTHER WENT TO BORNEO AND ALL I GOT WAS THIS T-SHIRT. Tears pricked her eyes.

Her best friend, Missy, tried to cheer her up. "I have some extra barrettes in my desk," she said. "We can at least fix your hair."

Rose hesitated. Barrettes? She never wore barrettes. It just wasn't her style. "No, thank you, I—" she
began.

But Missy cut her off. "Do you want to look special
on Picture Day, or not?"

Rose nodded.

"Then come on," said Missy. She pulled Rose into a
corner of the room, right next to Mr. Jupiter's suit of
armor—"Found while exploring the underground
tomb of the Knights Templar," he had explained—and
began pinning plastic butterflies all over Rose's head.

At that moment, Amisha walked over. "You need
earrings, too," she said, and she clipped a dangly pair
onto Rose's earlobes.

Earrings? Rose never wore earrings. They weren't
her style either. Besides, they pinched. "I'd rather go
without jewelry," said Rose.

"No jewelry on Picture Day?" gasped Amisha. She
jangled her gold bracelets. "You wouldn't look special
enough."

Before Rose could reply, Victoria pushed her way
into the corner. "You, girl, need some color," she pro-
claimed. Whipping out a tube of Cha-Ching Cherry

lip gloss, she aimed it at Rose's mouth and said, "Pucker up."

"I don't know if this is such a good idea," said Rose. "I've never worn makeup before."

"That's obvious," replied Victoria. "Still, you want to look special on Picture Day, don't you?"

Rose nodded.

Victoria smeared a thick pink streak across Rose's mouth, then touched up her own shimmering lips. "Now we *both* look special."

Rose longed to wipe away the sticky mess, but before she could grab a tissue, Emberly slipped a pair of rhinestone sunglasses over her eyes.

"Now, *that* looks special," he declared.

Then Jackie draped a basketball jersey over her shoulders.

"Really special," she declared.

And Ham tied a bow tie around her neck.

"Really, *really* special," he declared.

"I don't know—" began Rose.

But her classmates paid no attention to her. They were too busy adding:

Knee pads.

A nose ring.

Tube socks.

Snow boots.

Press-on fingernails.

A cowboy hat.

A charm bracelet.

Temporary tattoos.

A sequined belt.

A silk scarf.

And a plastic Hawaiian lei.

At last they stepped back to admire their work.

"What do you think?" they asked Rose. They turned her so she could see her reflection in the suit of armor's shiny breastplate.

Rose gasped. None of it—not the tattoos or the boots or the nose ring—was her style. She looked—

"So, so special," sighed Missy.

The others nodded their agreement.

Rose looked from her ridiculous reflection to her smiling classmates. How could she tell them she thought she looked stupid?

She couldn't.

At that moment, Mr. Jupiter, dressed for the occasion in a Mayan ceremonial robe—"A gift from the

President of Mexico," he had explained—clapped his hands. "Line up, please. It's time for pictures."

Everyone hurried to the door.

Miserably, Rose followed.

In the lunchroom, Miss Turner was already in front of the camera. Or at least the fourth graders thought it was Miss Turner. In place of her usual shapeless jumper and bulky sweater, however, the librarian was wearing an attractive blue dress that showed off curves no one had ever known she had.

"Say 'cheese,'" said the photographer.

"Cheeeese," said Miss Turner, smiling.

Flash!

She wiggled her fingers at Mr. Jupiter before hurrying back to the library, her sensible loafers making their faint *shush-shush* sound.

Then it was Victoria's turn. Pinching her cheeks and biting her lips to make them redder, she smiled a dazzling smile.

Flash!

Emberly grinned from ear to ear.

Flash!

Lenny stuck out his tongue.

Flash!

Finally, Rose stepped gloomily in front of the camera.

"Smile," said the photographer.

"How can I?" she sighed. "Look what I'm wearing!"

The photographer shrugged.

Flash!

Rose couldn't smile for the class photo either. As she knelt in the front row—earrings pinching, tube socks falling down—she crossed her fingers. *Please, oh, please, let the camera break. Let the photographer accidentally cover the lens with his thumb. Let the photography studio lose the pictures. . . .*

Three weeks later, Mr. Jupiter announced, "Wonderful news, children. Your pictures are here." He began handing out envelopes.

Victoria ripped hers open. "Lovely, as usual," she purred.

"I look good too," said Bernadette.

"Boy, I'm handsome," said Melvin.

The others ignored him.

As for Rose, she held the envelope in her trembling hand. She couldn't bring herself to open it.

"Yowza!" yelped Humphrey. "Look at the class picture. Look at Rose."

Everyone but Rose pulled their class picture out of the envelope. She braced herself.

"Man, your hair looks like a bees' nest," snickered Ham.

"Like a butterflies' nest, actually," corrected Stanford.

"What's with the knee pads?" giggled Amisha.

"And the bow tie?" tittered Lil.

Then Mr. Jupiter shouted, "Stop!"

Everyone looked toward the teacher.

"I can't believe it!" he cried as he peered at the class picture. "How could this have happened? How? It simply will not do."

"What won't do?" asked Bernadette. "Rose's tattoo?"

"My outfit," explained Mr. Jupiter. "Don't you see? I wore a Mayan ceremonial robe without holding the matching canary-head scepter." He slapped his forehead. "In the tribal world, it's a complete fashion no-no. Well, there's nothing else to do. We'll have to retake the class photo."

"We will?" said Rose hopefully.

"Absolutely," replied Mr. Jupiter.

Rose smiled with relief.

"Want to borrow my butterfly barrettes again?" asked Missy.

"No, thanks," said Rose. And she smiled at her ordinary, everyday reflection in the breastplate of Mr. Jupiter's suit of armor.

MORAL: Try to please all, and you end by pleasing none.

DANCE, STANFORD, DANCE

TEACHERS CALLED STANFORD BINET conscientious. This meant he did all his homework, studied for every test, kept the inside of his desk tidy, and always returned his library books on time.

This also meant he annoyed his classmates.

"Why can't you act like a regular kid?" Calvin asked during Friday free time.

Stanford—who was alphabetizing next month's vocabulary words—snorted. "You mean waste my time like everyone else?" He rolled his eyes. "Get serious."

"I am serious," said Calvin. "You should play more games, have more fun, laugh once in a while."

Stanford snorted again. "Playing games won't earn me an A in spelling. Having fun won't make me the best student in the class. Laughing won't get me into a top-notch college."

"Geez," said Calvin, "who cares about stupid stuff like that?"

"I do," snapped Stanford. He went back to his alphabetizing.

Calvin went back to his finger paints.

Just then Mr. Jupiter clapped his hands. "Put away your things and line up at the door, please. It's time to rehearse for this year's fall musical."

"I hate the fall musical," Lenny grumbled as the children headed down the hall. "I always end up wearing a squirrel costume."

"Leonard," corrected Mr. Jupiter, "you know I don't allow that word. There is no hating in my classroom."

Lenny looked around. "I'm not hating in the classroom," he said. "I'm hating in the hallway."

"There is no hating in the hallway, either," said Mr. Jupiter.

The children walked into the auditorium.

"Can I hate in here?" asked Lenny.

Mr. Jupiter shook his head.

"I hate that," Lenny muttered under his breath. He followed the others onto the stage.

Mrs. Playwright, the traveling drama teacher, was waiting for them. Until this year, every elementary school had always had its own drama teacher. But the district had run out of money. Now all sixty-four elementary schools shared Mrs. Playwright.

She smiled. "I'm so excited about this year's fall musical at Marcus Aurelius Elementary School."

"Marcus Aurelius?" repeated Humphrey.

The children looked at one another.

"You mean Aesop Elementary School," said Amisha.

"What?" said Mrs. Playwright.

"This is Aesop School," said Bernadette.

"It is?" said Mrs. Playwright. She flipped open her calendar. "Let's see, Marcus Aurelius School on the sixth . . . Caesar School on the sixteenth . . . Ovid School on the twenty-sixth . . . Aesop School on the—" She turned back to the children. "I'm so excited about this year's fall musical at Aesop Elementary School."

She handed out sheets of music.

"Now then, children," she said, "this is the song you will be performing. Let's sing just the first verse so I know what you sound like. Ready?"

She tooted her pitch pipe, and the children squawked:

"Up on the treetops, I see leaves,
They are swaying in the breeze,
First they are green, but when it turns cold,
They change to red and orange and gold."

"Gag," said Calvin.

"Gross," said Emberly.

"Barf," said Mrs. Playwright. "That was awful. This class is going to need *lots* of singing practice. Now let's see your dancing skills. Your routine goes like this." She demonstrated:

"Side-together, clap!
Side-together, clap!
Shimmy, shuffle, hop, turn, kick!
Cha-cha-cha!

Now you try," she said.

The children hopped, shuffled, kicked . . .

"Omph!"

Amisha bumped into Ham.

Rachel tripped over Melvin.

Bruce accidentally grabbed Bernadette's hand.

"Cooties!" he cried.

"Get serious," snorted Stanford. "It's a scientific fact that girls don't have cooties."

"Then you won't mind if I do this," said Bruce. He wiped his hand on Stanford's Theory of Relativity T-shirt.

"Disgusting!" cried Stanford.

"I agree," said Mrs. Playwright. "Your dancing skills are disgusting. This class is going to need lots of dancing practice, too."

"How long do we have to learn it all?" Stanford asked.

"Just six weeks," answered Mrs. Playwright. "That means all of you will need to—"

"Get serious," said Stanford.

"Exactly," said Mrs. Playwright. She smiled at Stanford. "The fourth graders at Cicero Elementary School are certainly conscientious."

"Cicero Elementary School?" repeated Humphrey.

"You mean Aesop Elementary School," corrected Victoria.

"What?" said Mrs. Playwright.

"This is Aesop School," said Lil.

"Oh . . . right," said Mrs. Playwright. She shook her head to clear it. "The fourth graders here at Aesop Elementary are certainly conscientious."

"I try," said Stanford.

"I think I'm going to be sick," gagged Bruce.

After that, Stanford practiced every chance he got. He practiced on the playground.

"Up on the treetops . . ."

In the lunch line.

"I see leaves . . ."

Even in the boys' bathroom.

"They are swaying in the breeze . . ."

His classmates watched with annoyance.

"Why bother?" Bernadette asked one day. "The fall musical is a long way off."

"Get serious," said Stanford. "The day of the show will be here before you know it. I'm learning my part, and I think you should too."

But no one listened to his advice.

Three weeks before the musical, Stanford knew the entire song—all three verses—by heart.

The others knew nothing.

"Let's take it again from the top!" cried Mrs.

Playwright during rehearsal. She blew her pitch pipe and sang, *"Up on the treetops, I see—"*

"Fleas," sang Rose.

"A wet sneeze," sang Bruce.

"Limburger cheese," sang Ham.

"Get serious," said Stanford.

"Why?" replied his classmates. "We've still got plenty of time."

They kept rhyming.

Stanford kept practicing.

Two weeks before the musical, Stanford could do every kick, shimmy, and shuffle perfectly.

The others could do nothing.

"Show me your cha-cha-cha!" cried Mrs. Playwright during rehearsal.

Bernadette did two leaps and an arabesque.

Jackie spun around on her back.

Bruce grabbed Calvin and tangoed him around the stage.

"Get serious," said Stanford.

"We will," replied his classmates. "Later."

They all tangoed.

Stanford practiced.

One week before the musical, Stanford could sing

all three verses while kicking, shimmying, and shuffling at the same time.

As for the others?

"We'll start tomorrow," they said.

"You promise?" begged Mrs. Playwright.

"Cross our hearts and hope to cha-cha-cha," they replied.

Stanford rolled his eyes. "Get serious," he said. And he kept practicing.

When the night of the fall musical arrived, the auditorium was crammed full. Exhausted teachers, excited students, proud parents, bored brothers and sisters, crying babies, obligated school board members, aunts, uncles, grandparents, even a photographer from the local newspaper took up every seat.

Mrs. Playwright stepped into the spotlight. "Welcome to Petronius Elementary School's fall musical."

The audience looked at one another.

"You mean Aesop Elementary School," whispered Mrs. Struggles from the front row.

"What?" asked Mrs. Playwright.

"AESOP SCHOOL!" Mrs. Bunz bellowed through the bullhorn she always kept at her side.

"Is it?" asked Mrs. Playwright. She flipped open her calendar. "Let's see, Petronius on the fourth, Pliny the Elder on the fourteenth, Horace on the twenty-fourth, Aesop School on the—" She turned back to the audience. "Welcome to Aesop Elementary School's fall musical."

The audience clapped.

Backstage, the fourth graders watched nervously as the first graders brought down the house with their song "I'm a Little Acorn."

The second graders tickled the audience's funny bone with a humorous skit called "Roly-poly Pumpkin."

The third graders stopped the show with their interpretive dance "Make Applesauce."

Then it was the fourth graders' turn.

"Break a leg," said Mr. Jupiter.

"That's a terrible thing to say," said Missy.

"It's an expression I learned while performing in *Cats* on Broadway," explained Mr. Jupiter. "It's theater talk for 'good luck.'"

"Oh, in that case, thank you," said Missy.

"You're welcome," said Mr. Jupiter. He hurried off to take his seat in the audience.

"You're on," whispered Mrs. Playwright. She began pushing the children from the wings.

They stumbled onstage and into the spotlight.

"Now what?" whispered Lenny. He shoved the sagging hood of his squirrel costume out of his eyes just as the music started.

"Up on the treetops," the fourth graders began shakily, *"I see—"*

"LEAVES!" Stanford belted out.

Bursting from the wings, he whirled across the stage, his oak leaf costume fluttering behind him.

Bumping past Lenny—

"Oomph!"

elbowing aside Emberly—

"Ouch!"

tripping Victoria—

"Hey!"

he side-together, clapped, side-together, clapped as he sang:

"Up on the treetops I see leaves,
They are swaying in the breeze,
First they are green, but when it turns cold,
They change to red and orange and gold."

His classmates tried to keep up, but it was no use.
They kicked when they should have shimmied.
They shuffled when they should have kicked.
And no one knew when to cha-cha-cha.
Finally, they came to a complete standstill as
Stanford danced around them, then burst into the
second verse:

"Go! Go! Go!
Where did they go?
Ho! Ho! Ho!
Don't you know?"

The audience leaped to its feet as Stanford cha-cha-
chaed his way into the big finish.

"That's when the wind blows
Swish! Swish! Swish!

And they come floating
DOOOOOWN
LIIIIIKE
THIIIIIS!"

As the rest of the class slunk offstage, the audience whistled, stomped their feet, and shouted, "Encore! Encore!"

Mrs. Playwright asked Stanford to take a bow.

And the newspaper photographer snapped his picture. "Our readers want to know," he said. "Do you plan on becoming a singer and dancer when you grow up?"

Stanford snorted. "Get serious." Then he hurried offstage to work on his book report about *The Haunted Room* by Hugo First. After all, it was due in just six weeks.

MORAL: It is wise to prepare today for the wants of tomorrow.

CALVIN GOES TO KINDERGARTEN

IT WAS MATH TIME IN MR. JUPITER'S class.

"All right, students," said Mr. Jupiter. "You have two minutes to do your multiplication tests." He flipped over his hourglass—"Made from the sands of the Sahara Desert," he explained. "Ready . . . set . . . go."

The fourth graders attacked their papers. Most of them were already up to sixteens and seventeens. Emberly was on the twenty-nines. Stanford was on the thirty-fours.

Calvin Tallywong was still on the threes.

Calvin looked down at his test paper and started writing the answers.

$3 \times 1 = 3$. That was easy enough.

$3 \times 2 = 6$. That wasn't bad either.

But what about 3×7? Or 3×9? Or 3×12?

Calvin stuck his pencil in his mouth and gnawed at the eraser. He knew he shouldn't. He knew he was going to need that eraser very soon. But he couldn't help it. When he was nervous, he chewed. And multiplication made him very nervous.

3 x 3 = . . . um . . . um . . . 9? Yes, definitely . . . probably . . . maybe 9.

3 x 4 = 14? No, that didn't look right. He tried to erase the answer but ended up with a gooey, wet smear.

Calvin sighed. Even if he'd managed to learn the threes, there were still the fours to struggle through . . . and the sevens . . . and the nines . . . and . . . The numbers stretched to infinity. Calvin felt the weight of all those numbers pressing down on him. It felt like the weight of the world.

"Time!" called Mr. Jupiter. "Pass your tests forward, please."

Across the room, Calvin's best friend, Humphrey, punched his fist into the air. Calvin knew Humphrey had passed his fourteens.

Behind him, Stanford raised his hand. "Mr. Jupiter," he said, "I think I passed my thirty-fours. May I stay after school and do my thirty-fives and thirty-sixes?"

"Show-off," muttered Calvin under his breath. He chewed and swallowed more of his eraser.

Then he laid his head on his desk. "Why do I have

to be in fourth grade?" he moaned softly to himself. "It's too hard."

"Did you say something, Calvin?" asked Mr. Jupiter.

Calvin looked up and shook his head. But to himself he said, "I wish I was in kindergarten again, where school was fun and easy."

ZZZZZ-CRACK!

The loudspeaker buzzed and crackled. Then Mrs. Shorthand's disembodied voice filled the room. "Mr. Jupiter? Come in, Mr. Jupiter."

The class giggled. Before becoming the school secretary, Mrs. Shorthand had been an air traffic controller.

"I read you loud and clear, Mrs. Shorthand," said Mr. Jupiter. "Go ahead."

"Miss Fairchild needs a student helper in her kindergarten class on the double. Do you roger that?"

"I roger," replied Mr. Jupiter. "Help is on the way."

ZZZZZ-CRACK!

The loudspeaker buzzed and crackled off.

Mr. Jupiter looked out across his classroom. "Who would like to be a student helper this morning?"

"Me!" said Jackie.

"Me!" repeated Humphrey.

"Oooh!" grunted Ham. He stretched his hand toward the ceiling. "Oooh! Oooh!"

Mr. Jupiter looked past the boys. His gaze fell on Calvin, who was still resting his head and gnawing on his eraser. "Calvin, you may go to the kindergarten room. The rest of you, please take out your arithmetic books and turn to page one thousand and twenty-six."

Calvin took the pencil out of his mouth and tucked it into his shirt pocket. He walked down the hall to the kindergarten room.

The kindergartners were sitting on the carpet when he arrived. They turned to stare at him as he stepped through the door.

"I'm Calvin," said Calvin.

"Of course you are," chirped Miss Fairchild. A wide, white-toothed smile spread across her cheeks as she turned to her students and clap-clapped her hands. "Class, let's sing hello to Calvin."

Seventeen kindergartners burst into song.

> *"Hello,*
> *Hello, and how are you?*

We like you,
We like you,
And we hope you like us, too!"

Calvin's cheeks turned pink. "Um . . . I'm your helper," he explained.

"And such a *big* helper, too," said Miss Fairchild. "I bet you're the biggest kindergartner in the whole school."

"Uh . . . n-no . . . ," stammered Calvin. "I'm a fourth grader."

"Oh, you silly billy," said Miss Fairchild. "Class, isn't Calvin a silly billy?"

"YES!" chimed the class.

They all smiled at him.

Calvin suddenly felt very confused. And very nervous. He pulled out his pencil and chewed on the eraser.

"Oh, dear," said Miss Fairchild. "Boys and girls, can you tell Calvin our rule about pencils?"

"NO CHEWING!" they chimed.

Miss Fairchild beamed. "That's right. Chewing is for beavers. Now put your pencil away and come sit down."

For a second Calvin stood there, uncertain. Then

he shrugged. Circle time beat math time anytime. Sticking the pencil back in his pocket, he moved toward the carpet.

"Wait!" shrieked a little girl. "That boy isn't wearing a bus!" A yellow construction-paper bus hung from a string around her neck. It read EMILY. "He can't sit down if he's not wearing a bus."

"Yeah," said a boy whose bus identified him as Mikey. "He has to have a bus."

"That's okay," said Calvin. "I don't need a bus."

"Yes, you do," said Mikey. "That's the rule."

"Mikey's right, Calvin," chirped Miss Fairchild. "All kindergartners wear buses."

"But I'm a fourth grader," said Calvin.

Miss Fairchild didn't hear. She was too busy cutting a school bus out of yellow construction paper. "There, now, all this bus needs is a name. Can you spell your name?"

"Of course I can," said Calvin indignantly.

"What letter does it start with?" asked Miss Fairchild.

"*C*," said Calvin.

"*C!*" exclaimed Miss Fairchild. "What a wonderful letter! Class, can you make the sound of the letter *C*?"

Like a flock of crows, the kindergartners cried, "Caaa-caaa-caaa!"

Calvin felt his cheeks grow even hotter.

Miss Fairchild clap-clapped her hands. "Very good," she gushed. She wrote a big letter *C* on Calvin's school bus, then asked, "Do you know what letter comes next? Sound it out if you need to."

"*A,*" answered Calvin. "The next letter is *A,* followed by an *L* and a *V* and an *I* and an *N. Calvin.*"

Miss Fairchild beamed again. "Did you hear that, class? Calvin has learned to spell his name! Let's give him three cheers. Ready? Hip-hip—"

"HOORAY!" chimed the kindergartners.

"Hip-hip—"

"HOORAY!"

"Hip-hip—"

"HOORAY!"

Multiplication tables, thought Calvin, were starting to look good.

Miss Fairchild wrote the rest of Calvin's name on the bus, then tied a piece of yarn to it and draped it around his neck. "Now you may sit," she said.

He found a spot between a boy whose bus said RILEY and a girl whose bus said SYDNEY.

"Miss Fairchild," whined Mikey. "The new boy isn't using pretzel legs. He has to use pretzel legs. That's the rule."

"Mikey's right, Calvin," said Miss Fairchild. "All kindergartners use pretzel legs."

"But I'm a fourth grader," Calvin said again.

Miss Fairchild didn't hear. She was too busy opening a big book and setting it on the easel.

Calvin tucked up his legs and followed along as the class read *Chicka Chicka Boom Boom.* Calvin already knew the story, so it was easy.

Next, they recited the days of the week. That was easy too.

Even math time was easy.

"One cookie plus one cookie equals how many cookies, class?" asked Miss Fairchild.

The kindergartners were puzzled, but not Calvin. "Two!" he cried. "Two cookies."

"Very good!" gushed Miss Fairchild.

Calvin grinned. Math should always be this easy. School should always be this easy.

Then Miss Fairchild clap-clapped her hands again. "Boys and girls, let's end circle time with something special—the squirrel dance!"

Seventeen eager kindergartners leaped to their feet. Wrinkling their noses and wiggling their bottoms, they chanted:

> *"Gray squirrel,*
> *Gray squirrel,*
> *Swish your bushy tail.*
> *Gray squirrel,*
> *Gray squirrel,*
> *Swish your bushy tail.*
> *Wrinkle up your little nose,*
> *Hold a nut between your toes.*
> *Gray squirrel,*
> *Gray squirrel,*
> *Swish your bushy tail."*

Suddenly, Mikey pointed an accusing finger. "Miss Fairchild," he whined, "Calvin didn't swish his bushy tail. He has to swish his bushy tail. That's the rule."

All eyes fell on Calvin.

"But I'm too big to swish," said Calvin. "I'm in fourth grade."

Miss Fairchild didn't hear. "In kindergarten,

everyone swishes," she chirped. "Come on. Let's see your swish."

Calvin shook his head.

"Like this," said Miss Fairchild. She wiggled her ample bottom. "See?"

"No," said Calvin.

"Don't be shy," coaxed Miss Fairchild. "Just swish."

"Swish!" whined Mikey.

"Swish!" shrieked Emily.

"Swish! Swish! Swish!" chimed the rest of the class.

"We're not leaving the carpet until you do," chirped Miss Fairchild. She smiled encouragingly.

And Calvin gave in. *I hope Humphrey never finds out about this,* he thought as he wiggled his hips and wrinkled his nose and pretended to hold a nut. *I hope he never knows I swished my bushy tail.*

Thinking about Humphrey made Calvin wonder what the rest of his class was doing. Were they reviewing the times tables? Learning fractions? Doing advanced calculus? Calvin was pretty sure they weren't reciting the days of the week or doing the squirrel dance.

Maybe, thought Calvin, *kindergarten's a little too easy. Maybe—*

Miss Fairchild clap-clapped, interrupting his thoughts. "Snack time," she said. "Everyone take a seat at the tables."

Snack time?

All thoughts of fourth grade vanished as Calvin headed for the table. Avoiding the swish-demanding Mikey, he took a seat between a boy with a buzz cut whose school bus read VICTOR and a girl holding a bean-bag platypus. Her school bus said ALICIA.

Victor turned and stared at Calvin.

Calvin stared back.

Victor stuck a pudgy finger up his nostril.

Calvin looked away.

Miss Fairchild sang out, "Who wants a yummy cheese stick and a box of raisins?" She passed out the snack.

Victor took his finger out of his nose and stuck it into his box of raisins. "I'm picking a winner," he announced, and he pulled out a plump raisin. For one moment he balanced it on the very tip of his nose finger; then—

Pop!

Both finger and raisin went into his mouth.

Calvin shuddered.

Here was something that never happened in fourth grade.

"Peck-peck. Peck-peck." On his other side, Alicia made her beanbag platypus waddle across the table. It attacked Calvin's napkin with its little plastic bill. It lunged at his cheese stick. It nipped at his raisin box.

Here was something else that never happened in fourth grade.

The platypus whirled on Emily, sitting only a few seats away. "Peck-peck! Peck-peck!" It bit Emily's hand.

Emily started to cry.

Miss Fairchild rushed over. "Where are our table manners, children?" she asked. "Victor, no picking. Picking is for chickens. Alicia, no pecking. Pecking is for woodpeckers. And Emily?" She patted the sobbing girl's back. "There, there, it's not a real bill."

At the next table, Mikey leaped from his chair and started swishing again. But this time he wasn't doing the squirrel dance. He was doing the potty dance. "Miss Fairchild," he whined. "I have to go. I have to go bad. I have to—"

Uh-oh!

Disgusted, Calvin watched as a puddle formed around Mikey's left shoe.

Here was something else that definitely never happened in fourth grade.

Mikey's lips trembled. His eyes grew as wet as his pants. He started to cry.

Emily joined him, louder than before.

Victor stuck his finger back in his nose.

Alicia's platypus pecked Sydney.

And the girl sitting across from Calvin went berserk. "I want to go home. I want my mommy!"

"MOMMY! MOMMY!" chanted the rest of the class.

Next to Calvin, Victor calmly transferred his finger to the other nostril.

Help! thought Calvin. *I'm trapped in kindergarten!*

He imagined the peace and tranquillity of his fourth-grade classroom, everyone sitting quietly at their desk memorizing their multiplication tables. It was a beautiful thought.

"I wish I was in the fourth grade again," whispered Calvin.

ZZZZZ-CRACK!

"Miss Fairchild, come in, Miss Fairchild. Can you

55

send Calvin Tallywong to the fourth grade, please? Over and out."

Calvin didn't hesitate. He ripped off his school bus and ran for the door, down the hall, toward his own classroom. He was ready to tackle the threes . . . the fours . . . the multiplication tables into infinity. Nothing was too hard. No sirree.

Excitedly, Calvin burst through the door, then skittered to a stop. What was going on? Why was the whole class standing . . . and wrinkling their noses . . . and wiggling their bottoms?

Humphrey waved. "Hey, Calvin, you're just in time. Look what Mr. Jupiter taught us."

And as Calvin stood, openmouthed, his classmates chanted:

"Gray squirrel,
Gray squirrel,
Swish your bushy tail."

MORAL: Be careful what you wish for—it might come true.

THE BOY WHO CRIED LUNCH MONITOR

MRS. BUNZ RULED AESOP ELEMENTARY'S lunchroom with an iron fist. No kid dared blow bubbles in his milk, or slurp her spaghetti, or stick a straw up his nose. If one of them did . . .

"LUNCHROOM INFRACTION!" Mrs. Bunz would bellow through her bullhorn. "Five minutes . . . *on the wall!*"

On the wall. Those three words struck fear into the heart of every student at Aesop Elementary—first graders and fifth graders alike.

On the wall. It was Mrs. Bunz's favorite punishment— a form of torture so horrible that anyone who endured it never again left his bread crusts uneaten, or chewed with her mouth open.

Still, at the beginning of every school year, there was always one kid foolish enough to tangle with Big Bad Bunz.

"You know what I'm having for lunch?" that kid might holler. And before anyone could warn her, she would open her mouth wide so all could see the glob of half-chewed baloney with mustard and pickle relish on pumpernickel lurking inside, and she would squeal, "SEAFOOD!"

The lunch monitor's vengeance was swift. "LUNCHROOM INFRACTION!" Mrs. Bunz would bellow. "Five minutes . . . *on the wall.*"

The other students would shudder.

Mrs. Bunz made the kid face the room with her back to the cold tiled wall. "I think you have something to say to your schoolmates," she would growl.

"Huh?" The kid always looked bewildered.

"An apology," Mrs. Bunz would continue. "You owe us all an apology."

No one could bear to watch. One hundred elementary school students would quickly look down at their carrot sticks or stare at their orange slices.

"I . . . I don't understand." The kid was always red-faced and stammering by this time. Waves of humiliation were washing over her. She was drowning in them.

That was when Mrs. Bunz would pull the note card from her pocket. Yellowed with age and wrinkled from much use, it had, through the years, been held in the quaking hands of dozens of students. Now it was this kid's turn.

"Read it," Mrs. Bunz would say.

The kid recognized defeat. In a small, quavering voice—so unlike the voice that only moments earlier had shouted "SEAFOOD!"—she read, "I apologize for my rudeness and promise to use my best table manners the next time I sit down to lunch."

"Thank you," Mrs. Bunz would say. Then she'd walk away, leaving the kid to simmer in her own embarrassment for five long minutes . . . *on the wall.*

No wonder the children in Aesop Elementary's lunchroom sat up straight, ate in silence, and cleaned up all their trash.

"But," asked Mr. Jupiter one day as he bit into the cook's liverwurst-and-cranberry-sauce sandwich, "are the children happy? Do they enjoy lunchtime?"

"Lunchtime isn't about enjoyment," Mrs. Bunz replied. "It's about discipline, and maintaining order."

At that moment, Mrs. Struggles raced into the lunchroom.

"Bertha, come quick," she panted. "There's a traffic jam in the kindergarten drop-off lane. I need you and your bullhorn to untangle it."

"I'm on my way!" cried Mrs. Bunz. She rushed from the lunchroom.

Mr. Jupiter followed.

Left unmonitored, the students sat in silence for a moment. Then—

Rose cautiously leaned over and whispered in Missy's ear.

Emberly quietly offered Ham a chocolate chip cookie.

Lenny glanced furtively around the lunchroom. Then he took a big swig of his Mr. Fizz and—

"B-U-U-U-R-P!"

The doors of restraint were belched wide open.

Jackie wildly pitched Cheesy Puffs into Calvin's open mouth.

Ashlee A., Ashleigh B., and Ashley Z. put their mashed potatoes together and built a snowman.

Amisha gargled with chocolate milk.

The only fourth grader not laughing or talking or joining in the fun was Melvin Moody.

Melvin was used to not joining in. He was used to not being a part of the group. Somehow, in Mr. Jupiter's class, Melvin always managed to blurt out the wrong thing, or pick his nose when someone was looking, or fumble the ball at recess and lose the championship kickball game. This kind of behavior tended to keep other kids away.

Now Melvin was suddenly seized with an uncontrollable urge.

Leaping to his feet, he cupped his hands around his mouth and cried, "Lunch monitor! Lunch monitor!"

Fear swept through the room.

Pretzels were yanked from nostrils.

Bread crusts were swallowed whole.

The entire student body smoothed their hair, sat up straight, and hoped their cheeks weren't too flushed with joy.

A minute passed.

Then another.

And another.

"She's not coming," Victoria finally said.

Lenny whirled on Melvin. "You did it!" he shouted. "You ruined the fun."

All eyes turned to Melvin. Jackie booed. Rachel and Lil stuck out their tongues. Bruce threw a banana peel. It hit Melvin in the back of the head.

And Melvin loved it!

I'm the center of attention, he thought. He held his chin high.

For days afterward, Melvin felt like a celebrity.

"There's that kid from the lunchroom," whispered Bernadette.

"What a loser," whispered Ham.

"What's his name again?" asked Lil.

The others shrugged.

All too soon, however, Melvin's celebrity faded. By week's end, he was nobody again.

That was when Miss Turner wobbled into the lunchroom. Instead of her sensible *shush*ing shoes she was wearing a very spiky, very strappy, very purple pair of high-heeled sandals.

"Bertha," said Miss Turner, swaying slightly. "You've got a phone call in the office."

"I'm busy," grumbled Mrs. Bunz. Eyes narrowed, she plucked a recyclable can from the regular trash, then looked around for the rule breaker.

"But it's your mother, the marine," said Miss Turner. She grabbed the edge of a nearby table to steady herself. "She's calling from boot camp."

Mrs. Bunz hesitated, then dropped the can into the recycling bin and headed for the office.

At that moment, Miss Turner spied Mr. Jupiter giving the cook a recipe for yak and cheese. "A delicacy among the nomads of the Gobi Desert," he said.

She took a wobbly step toward him and—

"Ooops!" said Mr. Jupiter. He caught the librarian before she hit the floor. "One must be careful when wearing such lofty shoes."

Miss Turner melted into his arms. "Dear me," she sighed weakly. "I think I've twisted my ankle."

"Allow me to help you back to the library," offered Mr. Jupiter.

They limped away, leaving the lunchroom—unmonitored!

Within seconds—

First graders crawled under tables.

Second graders squeezed the cream filling out of their cupcakes.

Third graders blew bits of fruit cocktail from their straws.

As for the fourth graders, they raced their sandwich cookies down the length of the table.

"And Oreo takes the lead," said Jackie in her sports announcer voice, "followed by Hydrox and Girl Scout. . . ."

Then—

"Lunch monitor! Lunch monitor!" Melvin cried.

Quick as a wink, straws were stuck back into milk cartons.

Sandwich cookies were popped into mouths.

Flushed and panting, everyone braced themselves for . . . nothing!

"Not again," moaned Calvin. He whirled on Melvin. "What's your problem, kid?"

But Melvin didn't have a problem, because once again, in the days that followed, he was talked about . . . recognized . . . SOMEBODY!

Fame was fleeting. By the middle of the following week, Melvin was as forgotten as last month's vocabulary words.

That was when, during lunch—

CRASH!

"Argh!"

"Mayday!" cried Mrs. Shorthand, who had been

standing on a swivel chair and hanging a sign in the hallway. "Mayday!"

Mrs. Bunz rushed to help her.

Left alone in the lunchroom, the students didn't waste a second.

Everyone laughed, or joked, or blew milk out their nose.

At the fourth-grade table, Jackie had invented a game called Flick Your Pea, and everyone was playing. Everyone, that is, except Melvin.

Then he saw her—Mrs. Bunz—coming down the hallway, closer and closer.

"Lunch monitor! Lunch monitor!" he cried.

"Yeah, right," drawled Lenny. He flicked a pea into Missy's applesauce.

Mrs. Bunz reached the door.

Melvin hopped up and down. He waved his arms. He cried even more loudly, "Lunch monitor! Lunch monitor!"

"Knock it off, kid," said Calvin. "Nobody believes you." He aimed a pea at Stanford.

Mrs. Bunz pushed on the wide swinging doors.

Panicked and desperate, Melvin leaped onto the

fourth-grade table. He hopped up and down, waved his arms, and cried at the top of his voice, "Lunch monitor! Lunch monitor!"

His behavior finally grabbed their attention. Everyone stopped joking and laughing and flicking peas. They turned to look at Melvin just as Mrs. Bunz burst into the lunchroom.

"LUNCHROOM INFRACTION!" she bellowed through her bullhorn. Her eyes narrowed at the sight of Melvin, who was still hopping, waving, and shouting on top of the table.

"Unbelievable!" she said. "I'm gone just a few moments and look how you behave! Melvin Moody, that's five minutes . . . *on the wall.*"

MORAL: Liars are not believed even when they tell the truth.

PLEASE DON'T TEASE ASHLEY Z.

THERE WERE THREE ASHLEYS IN MR. Jupiter's class: Ashlee A., Ashleigh B., and Ashley Z.

Ashlee A. and Ashleigh B. liked to braid each other's hair, collect unicorns, and do cheers during class kickball games.

Ashley Z., on the other hand, liked to play in the dirt, collect bottle caps, and burp the alphabet. This was hardly surprising. After all, Ashley Z. was a boy.

"And don't you forget it!" he had hollered just that morning.

As usual, the other boys in the class had started the day by making fun of his name.

"Don't you belong over there?" Humphrey had asked when Ashley lined up at the water fountain. "That's the girls' line."

It was an old joke, but it still made Ashley boil. "Oh, yeah, you're really funny, Parrot," he retorted. He stomped away as the others hooted with laughter.

But the teasing continued.

At lunchtime, Emberly said, "Mrs. Bunz likes the

girls best. Her favorites are Ashlee A., Ashleigh B., and Ashley Z." Then he slapped his forehead dramatically. "Oh, wait a minute. You're not a girl, are you, Ashley?"

Ashley clenched his fists. "I'm also not a big jerk, like some people I know." Pushing away from his peanut butter and pickle sandwich, he stalked off.

"Hey!" Ham called after him as the others howled with laughter. "Are you going to eat that?"

Ashley was too mad to answer.

That afternoon the children played Fact-a-Rama, a game Mr. Jupiter had invented to help them review what they had learned during the week. Today it was boys versus girls, and Bernadette was up first.

"Give me a sentence with the words *defense, defeat,* and *detail* in it," said Mr. Jupiter.

Bernadette thought a moment, then answered, "When a horse jumps over *defense, defeat* go before *detail.*"

"Correct," said Mr. Jupiter. "One point for the girls."

The girls, especially Ashlee A. and Ashleigh B., cheered.

Mr. Jupiter turned to the boys' team. Calvin was next.

"If you add 34,317 to 76,188, divide the answer by 3, and multiply by 4, what do you get?"

"The wrong answer," said Calvin.

"Yes," said Mr. Jupiter. "That is exactly what you get. One point for the boys."

The boys pumped their fists victoriously and barked like dogs.

Missy was next.

"What nursery rhyme dates back to the Great Plague of London in 1664?"

"Easy," answered Missy. "'Ring Around the Rosy.'"

Mr. Jupiter nodded. But before he could award the girls a point, Lenny, Bruce, and Humphrey joined hands and danced around Ashley Z. They sang:

> *"Ring around the rosy,*
> *A pocketful of posies,*
> *The Ashleys! The Ashleys!*
> *They all wear gowns!"*

The children shrieked with laughter.

"Stop it!" cried Ashley.

But they couldn't.

Bruce high-fived Lenny. "Oh, man," he hooted, "we really burned him that time."

That was when Mr. Jupiter roared, "ENOUGH! EVERYONE SIT DOWN."

The children sat.

Mr. Jupiter looked at them with disappointment. "You know I do not allow teasing in my classroom."

"You don't?" said Melvin.

The others ignored him.

"I do not condone name-calling," Mr. Jupiter continued.

"Mr. Jupiter's such a Goody Two-shoes," Missy whispered to Rose.

"Or insults . . ."

"Party pooper," muttered Victoria under her breath.

"Or playing mean jokes."

"Is that practical?" asked Stanford.

"Besides," Mr. Jupiter went on, "there's nothing funny about the name Ashley. Did you know that in the Scottish village of Dun-Derry-Doody, where I once worked as a bagpipe tuner, every firstborn son is named Ashley? It means *from the ash tree*."

"Really?" said Lenny. "Did you know that here in the United States every firstborn *daughter* is named Ashley? It means *what a sissy*."

The children laughed again.

And Ashley Z. jumped up from his chair. "I'm going

to pound you, Lenny Wittier!" he cried. "I'm going to mash your face."

"Calm down," said Mr. Jupiter.

"No!" yelled Ashley. "I won't calm down! I'm tired of being laughed at! I'm tired of being teased!"

"Of course you are," soothed Mr. Jupiter. He wrapped his arm around the boy's heaving shoulders.

"Geez, Ashley," said Lenny. "Why are you acting like such a sissy? I was just joking around."

"It's not funny!" hollered Ashley.

Mr. Jupiter frowned at Lenny. "I don't want to hear another word out of you, Leonard. We'll talk about this *after* school."

Then he turned back to Ashley. "Why don't you go get a cool drink from the water fountain?"

"Okay," said Ashley in an anger-choked voice. Shooting Lenny one last poisonous look, he stormed out the door.

But the minute he was in the hall, furious tears filled his eyes. Wasn't there any way to make his classmates stop teasing him? Was he doomed to be kidded about his name forever?

He rounded the corner and—

"Good to see ya, kid," growled a deep voice.

Ashley looked up. He gulped, paled, gave a little groan.

There—just a few feet away—stood Tommy "Tarantula" Santangelo.

Every kid at Aesop Elementary School knew Tarantula, and every kid avoided him like the cook's tuna-oatmeal mush. No trick was too mean for the fifth grader. He shook down kindergartners for their milk money, knocked first graders off slides, and tossed second graders' book reports into mud puddles—all for the fun of it! Known for a teasing tongue as sharp as Miss Turner's stiletto heels, Tarantula stood six feet tall and had fists as big as Ham.

Ashley knew he was in trouble.

He turned to run.

"Hey, kid," called Tarantula in an attempt to stop him. "Come closer, huh?"

Ashley vigorously shook his head.

"C'mon, I won't hurt ya. I need your help. Look." Tarantula pointed to the seat of his nylon sweatpants. They were caught in a locker door.

"Help me out, will ya, kid?" said Tarantula.

Was this a trap? Ashley wondered. Some big joke to humiliate him even more? "Why should I?" he asked.

"Because I'll pound you if you don't," snarled Tarantula.

With a squeak, Ashley backed away.

"No, wait," Tarantula called. "I was just kidding! I didn't mean it, honest."

The desperate tone in the bully's voice made Ashley stop.

"Please, kid," begged Tarantula. "I can't let anybody see me like this."

Ashley kept his distance. "Why?" he asked.

Tarantula suddenly looked sheepish. "If the other fifth graders catch me here, I'll never hear the end of it," he admitted. "See? I got hooked on Sandy Pepperdine's locker."

"Huh?" said Ashley.

Tarantula blushed. "Look, I snuck away from gym class so I could slip a love note into Sandy's locker, and . . . well . . . this happened. If I don't get unstuck before gym class ends, I'm going to be the laughingstock of my class."

"I know how that feels," said Ashley. He took a few cautious steps forward.

From down the hall came the shrill sound of Mrs. Gluteal's whistle. "Fifth grade, line up," she hollered.

Tarantula tugged frantically at his pants. "They're coming!" he cried.

Ashley stepped a little closer.

The gym door swooshed open.

"Hurry," begged Tarantula.

Ashley stepped even closer.

He could hear the fifth graders shuffling down the hall now.

"Ah, man," moaned Tarantula. "I'm going to get teased, and if I'm teased, I'll end up pounding someone, and if I pound someone, I'll end up in Mrs. Struggles' office for who knows how long. I hate being teased."

"Me too," agreed Ashley. And quicker than Mr. Jupiter's light-year calculator ("Given to me by my friends at NASA," he had explained), the boy reached forward and freed Tarantula's pants from the locker door.

At that moment, the fifth graders turned the corner and swarmed around them.

"What's going on here, Mr. Santangelo?" the fifth-grade teacher, Mr. Lipschitz, asked suspiciously.

Tarantula plastered a smile onto his face. "Nothing, Mr. Lipschitz. I'm just have a chat with my good friend . . . um . . . uh . . . ."

"Ashley," said Ashley.

"Ashley?" repeated Tarantula.

Ashley nodded.

And Tarantula grinned. "I'll see you later . . . *Ashley*," he drawled.

I'm doomed, thought the fourth grader. *First my classmates, and now Tarantula. Life is so unfair.*

He shuffled back to his classroom.

The next morning before school, Calvin tapped Ashley Z. on the back. "I found this mermaid barrette underneath the monkey bars," he said, grinning. "Do you want it?"

Ashley tried to keep his cool. "Come on, you guys," he said. "You heard Mr. Jupiter. No teasing in the classroom."

"But this isn't the classroom," replied Lenny. "This is the playground." He smirked. "Have you heard the one about the pigtailed Ashley who—"

A sudden shadow blocked the sun.

The boys looked up.

They gulped, paled, gave a little groan.

"H . . . h . . . hi, Tarantula," stammered Ashley. He braced himself for the teasing that was sure to come.

"Don't call me Tarantula ever again," snarled the fifth grader. "I'm using a new nickname now."

"You are?" Ashley squeaked. "Wh . . . wh . . . what is it?"

"Ashley," said the fifth grader.

"Ashley?" repeated Humphrey.

"Uh-huh," said the fifth grader. His eyes narrowed, and his lips twisted into a sneer. "And from now on, anytime I hear someone making fun of the name Ashley, I'm gonna figure you're teasing *me*."

"Wh . . . wh . . . who'd make fun of the name Ashley?" sputtered Bruce.

"N . . . n . . . not me," added Lenny.

"I think it's a really c . . . c . . . cool name," said Calvin.

The boys scattered.

Ashley watched them go and smiled. "Thanks, Tarantula," he said.

"No sweat, kid," replied the bully. With a wink, he sauntered off to scare some third graders.

And Ashley sauntered off to his classroom.

MORAL: One good turn deserves another.

PFFFT!

RACHEL PIFFLE WAS THE QUIETEST GIRL
in fourth grade. She spoke so softly that no one—not
her teachers, her classmates, or even her parents—had
ever really heard her voice. For this reason, she was often overlooked.

On Tuesday morning, Mr. Jupiter asked, "Is anyone absent?"

The students looked around.

"Rachel is," Missy finally said.

Rachel, who was sitting at her desk, said softly,
"Pffft!"

No one heard her.

"Anyone else?" asked Mr. Jupiter.

The students looked around again.

"Just Rachel," said Emberly.

"Pffft!" Rachel said again.

Mr. Jupiter wrote Rachel's name on the attendance
slip. "Ashleigh B.," he said, "will you take this to the
office?"

Rachel tried one last time. "Pffft!"

No one heard her.

Mr. Jupiter clapped his hands. "Everyone line up, please. It's time for music."

Rachel loved music. "Pffft!" she said joyfully.

No one heard her.

In the music room, Mr. Halfnote passed out instruments.

A triangle for Ashley Z.

A tambourine for Bernadette.

A slide trombone for Stanford.

"Pffft!" said Rachel.

Mr. Halfnote didn't hear her.

Rachel helped herself to a pair of cymbals.

"Today," said the music teacher, "we will accompany ourselves as we sing 'The Battle Hymn of the Republic.'"

In the back row, Rachel shivered in anticipation. Music time was the only time she felt free to raise her voice.

Mr. Halfnote tapped his baton on his music stand. "Instruments up," he said. He held his hands in the air like a conductor. "And a one . . . and a two . . . and a you-know-what-to-do." He gave the downbeat.

Calvin pumped his accordion.

Victoria strummed her zither.

Melvin rang his cowbell.

The class sang out, *"Mine eyes have seen the glory . . ."*

Confident that no one could hear her above all the racket, Rachel banged her cymbals together and bellowed, *"HIS TRUTH IS MARCHING ON-N-N-N!"* It felt marvelous.

When they got to the song's end, Mr. Halfnote hollered, "Big finish!" He waved his baton wildly in the air, then pointed it at Jackie, who was playing the kettledrum.

Jackie put all her heart—and muscle—into it. She pounded the drum. She pummeled the drum. She—

"Heads up!" she yelped as one of the clublike drumsticks flew from her grasp and whistled through the air.

It bounced off Ham's forehead—

"Yeeeow!"

bashed into Bruce's upper lip—

"Ouch!"

ricocheted off Lil's elbow—

"Owie!"

banged into Missy's tummy—

"Ooomph!"

glanced off Rose's knee—

"Yowza!"

bopped into Victoria's backside—

"Waaah!"

smashed Bernadette's pinkie—

"Oooh-oooh! Aaah-aaah!"

and rolled to a stop at Rachel's feet.

So lost in the music was Rachel that she didn't notice the flying drumstick, her wounded classmates, or the fact that everyone else had stopped singing and playing their instrument. Instead, with eyes squeezed shut, she belted out, *"GLORY! GLORY! HALLELUJAH!"*

The others couldn't believe their ears. Rachel Piffle was—

"Are you okay?" cried Amisha.

"She must be hurt if she's screaming like that," Emberly said to Bernadette.

Melvin shook his head in confusion. "When did Rachel get here?"

The others ignored him.

Dropping their instruments, everyone raced to her side.

At that moment, Rachel opened her eyes . . . and turned as red as Mr. Jupiter's Japanese kimono.

"Are you bleeding?" asked Victoria. She rubbed her bruised backside.

"Pffft," Rachel said softly.

"How many fingers am I holding up?" asked Bruce. He dabbed at his swollen lip.

"Pffft," Rachel said.

"Speak to me," begged Ham. "Speak to me." He swiped a trickle of blood from his forehead.

"Pffft," Rachel said.

"The nurse!" cried Mr. Halfnote. "We have to get her to the nurse!"

Rachel's cymbals crashed to the floor as the music teacher flung her over his shoulder and dashed down the hall to Nurse Betadine's office. Bruised and bleeding, the others staggered behind.

"Tell me where it hurts," said Nurse Betadine after Rachel had been placed on the cot.

"Pffft!" Rachel said.

Nurse Betadine applied a compress to Rachel's forehead, an ice pack to her knee, and a splint to her pinkie.

"Will she be okay?" asked Lil, massaging her throbbing elbow.

"I don't know." Nurse Betadine frowned with

worry. Popping a thermometer into Rachel's mouth, she shooed the others back to their classroom.

Alone with her patient, the nurse began to fret. "Does she need an ambulance?" she asked herself.

"Pffft!"

"A hospital?"

"PFFFT!"

"A surgeon?"

"PFFFT!"

Finally, as a last resort, the nurse unwrapped a Band-Aid and stuck it on Rachel's backside.

"PFFFT! PFFFT! PFFF . . . FFF . . . FFF . . . FEEL GOOD! I FEEL GOOD!" Rachel sang out.

Nurse Betadine looked startled, then smiled. "I knew you would," she said. "Those Band-Aids work every time." And she sent Rachel back to her classroom.

Minutes later, Rachel took her seat behind Victoria.

"I hope Rachel's okay," Victoria said. She pressed a wet paper towel to her bruised backside.

"Pffft," Rachel said.

"I hope she doesn't miss too much school," said Bruce. He dabbed the blood from his lip with a tissue.

"Pffft," Rachel said.

"Maybe we should send flowers," said Rose. She wrapped an elastic bandage around her stiff knee.

"Pffft," Rachel said. "Daisies would be nice."

Ham looked up. "I think I'm hearing voices," he said. Rubbing his bruised forehead, he added, "I think we should send her some daisies."

"Good idea," agreed Lil.

"Pffft," Rachel said.

MORAL: The squeaky wheel gets the grease.

THERE ONCE WAS A MAN FROM DANCART...

LIL DITTY WAS THE MOST POETIC GIRL at Aesop Elementary School.

"'Ode to a Popsicle,'" Lil announced at recess one morning after finding a discarded stick on the tetherball court. And while Jackie and Calvin waited impatiently for her to move so that they could play, she recited:

> *"O empty stick*
> *stained with orange memory,*
> *you lie abandoned.*
> *Once full of licks,*
> *now full of ants,*
> *you—"*

THUMP!

"Oops," said Jackie, grinning. "Sorry."

"Ignoramus," huffed Lil, rubbing the side of her head.

"Whatever," said Jackie. And she served the ball.

* * *

That afternoon Mr. Jupiter made an exciting announcement.

"Today we will be beginning our poetry unit. Everyone, please open your *Language Arts for Dummies* books to page eight hundred thirty-seven."

"Hooray!" clapped Lil.

"Argh," moaned the rest of the class.

For the next half hour, Mr. Jupiter talked about haiku, sonnets, and limericks.

"I know a limerick!" cried Lenny. He recited:

> *"There once was a man from Dancart,*
> *Went to dinner with his dear sweetheart,*
> *At the table he burped,*
> *He belched and he slurped*
> *Even worse, he started to—"*

"Ahem!" Mr. Jupiter coughed loudly. "Thank you for that . . . ah . . . inspirational poem, Leonard."

Lenny grinned.

"Now then, class," said Mr. Jupiter. "We are going to have a contest."

"A contest?" cried Jackie. "What kind of contest?

Baseball? Basketball? Tetherball?" She flexed a well-developed bicep.

"Is it a beauty contest?" asked Victoria. She flipped her golden hair.

"Or a pie-eating contest?" asked Ham. He smacked his lips. "Is it? Huh?"

"No," answered Mr. Jupiter, "it's a poetry contest. If everyone memorizes at least twenty lines of poetry, we will have a class pizza party."

Ham smacked his lips again. "Make mine pepperoni."

Mr. Jupiter laughed. "You know, when I taught at the Botswana Middle School, my students' favorite topping was ostrich and mushroom, but . . ." He shook his head. "I digress. What was I talking about?"

"Poetry," said Bernadette.

"And pizza," added Ham.

"Right," said Mr. Jupiter. "Everyone has a chance to win pizza, but the student who memorizes the most lines of poetry wins . . ." He held up a book. *"This."*

In the front row, Lil squealed. "It's Emily Dickinson! *The Complete Works of Emily Dickinson!*"

"Emily who?" asked Rose.

"You know," said Lil. *" 'I'm nobody! Who are you? Are you—Nobody—too?' "*

"I'm somebody," said Rose. "Speak for yourself."

"Actually," said Mr. Jupiter, "Lil was reciting a poem written by Emily Dickinson."

"The world's greatest poet," Lil gushed.

Jackie's hand shot into the air. "Mr. Jupiter," she said, "this contest isn't fair."

"Why not?" asked Mr. Jupiter.

"Because Lil already knows lots of poems. She has an advantage."

"But when we run relay races, or play kickball, you have the advantage," Mr. Jupiter pointed out.

"That's different," said Jackie.

"How?" asked Mr. Jupiter.

Before Jackie could answer, Miss Turner stuck her curly blond head into the classroom.

Curly? Blond?

The fourth graders gasped. Miss Turner had gotten a new hairdo and—

"She looks fabulous," said Victoria under her breath.

"Mr. Jupiter, may I speak with you in the hall for a moment?" Miss Turner asked in a breathy voice.

"But of course," replied Mr. Jupiter. He stepped out into the hallway.

The moment he was gone, Lil turned around in her

seat. She stuck out her tongue at Jackie. "You're just mad because you know I'm going to win," she said. "And you can't stand to lose anything, not even a poetry contest."

Jackie felt her cheeks turning hot. "Who cares about winning a poetry contest anyway?" she asked. "Poetry's stupid."

"Maybe it's not the poetry that's stupid," Lil shot back.

"Ooooh," whistled Emberly. "That stings."

Jackie's cheeks burned.

"Ignoramus," hissed Lil.

"Come on, Jackie," urged Bernadette. "You can't let Little Miss Sonnet get away with that."

Jackie's cheeks were positively on fire.

"You might be able to dribble a ball," Lil went on, "but you can't memorize a ballad."

Jackie erupted. "Yes, I can!" She pointed her finger at Lil. "I challenge you to a race—a poetry race!"

"You're on," said Lil.

For the rest of the afternoon, the fourth graders worked on the thermometer graphs they would use to record the number of lines they memorized and recited.

Lil cut and pasted and hummed.

Jackie cut and pasted and moaned. What had she been thinking? How could she ever beat Lil?

The next afternoon, Mr. Jupiter asked, "Does anyone have a poem they would like to recite?"

"I do!" cried Lil. "It's called 'I Wandered Lonely as a Cloud,' and it was written by William Wordsworth, and"— she smirked at Jackie—"it's twenty-four lines long." Then, crossing her hands over her stomach, she recited:

> *"I wandered lonely as a cloud*
> *That floats on high o'er vales and hills,*
> *When all at once I saw a crowd,*
> *A host, of golden daffodils . . ."*

The poem went on and on.

At her desk, Jackie groaned. She didn't get it. What was the point? Why was a cloud lonely? Why was poetry so hard to understand?

"Word perfect," said Mr. Jupiter when Lil finished. "Does anyone else have a poem today?" He looked straight at Jackie.

Jackie slipped down in her chair. She had meant to have one, but the words refused to stick in her head.

All those lines! All those stanzas! Jackie hadn't known where to start memorizing.

It would help if poems were written about something interesting, she thought. But no. They all had to be about stupid stuff—clouds and loneliness and things that didn't make any sense.

"Anyone else?" asked Mr. Jupiter.

A few kids raised their hands.

As they recited, Lil turned to look at Jackie. "Loser," she mouthed.

Not if I can help it, vowed Jackie.

Jackie rushed to the library after school.

"You have to help me," she begged Miss Turner. "I feel like it's the ninth inning, I'm down ten runs, and I already have two outs."

The librarian nodded her understanding. "I think I have just the poem for you." Pulling a thick book off the shelf, she opened it to the last page.

Jackie looked at the poem and gasped. "It must be fifty lines long!"

"Fifty-eight, to be exact," replied Miss Turner.

Fifty-eight? A poem that long might just beat Lil's total. All she had to do was—

Jackie glanced at the poem again, and her heart sank. "How am I going to memorize all that?" she sighed.

"You can't win with no one on base," replied Miss Turner. "You have to take it one hit at a time."

"Or," said Jackie with dawning understanding, "one *line* at a time."

All week, Jackie worked on the poem—slowly, steadily.

By Wednesday she'd memorized six lines.

By Thursday she'd memorized ten lines.

By Friday she was a nervous wreck.

Everyone was racking up lines of poetry— everyone but her.

Victoria recited "Pippa's Song," by Robert Browning:

"The year's at the spring
and day's at the morn . . ."

Amisha recited "Louder Than a Clap of Thunder," by Jack Prelutsky:

"Louder than a clap of thunder,
louder than an eagle screams . . ."

Bruce recited the Blasto Bubble Gum jingle:

> *"Very chewy berry,*
> *Pop!*
> *Sticky in your hairy,*
> *Glop!"*

But Mr. Jupiter said that didn't count.
And every afternoon, Lil stood and recited a poem.
"Roses," by George Eliot.

> *"You love the roses—so do I. I wish*
> *the sky would rain down roses . . ."*

"The Eclipse," by Richard Eberhart.

> *"I stood out in the open cold*
> *To see the essence of the eclipse . . ."*

And "Do Not Go Gentle into That Good Night," by
Dylan Thomas:

> *"Do not go gentle into that good night,*
> *Old age should burn and rave at close of day . . ."*

"What's that about, huh?" said Ham.

"Death," replied Stanford. "What else?"

"Blech," gagged Ham.

By Friday, Lil's poetry score stood at fifty-six lines. Jackie's was zero.

After school, Lil loudly announced, "This contest is soooo booooring! There's just no competition."

Her friends, Ashlee A. and Ashleigh B., glanced at Jackie and giggled. Jackie's jaw tightened.

"After all," Lil went on, "everyone knows I can run rings around you-know-who when it comes to poetry."

The girls giggled again.

Jackie's fists clenched.

"Why, I'm so much better, I could win this race without reciting another line of poetry," declared Lil.

The Ashleys giggled a third time.

And Jackie exploded. "Try it!" she cried.

"I will," said Lil, and smiling smugly, she sauntered away.

All weekend, Jackie worked on the poem—slowly, steadily.

She skipped bowling practice and memorized six lines.

She skipped a gymnastics meet and memorized seven more lines.

She even skipped watching *Wrestle-Dementia* on television and memorized ten more lines.

By Monday morning, she knew half the poem by heart.

But she still had a long way to go.

The shot clock's ticking, she told herself. *I need to score. . . .*

She stole peeks at the poem during social studies.

She muttered snatches of it during spelling.

She recited it in her head during hula dancing.

By Friday afternoon, she was still seven lines short.

"Any poems?" Mr. Jupiter asked.

Hands around the room shot up.

But not Lil's. All week she had lounged confidently in her chair, smiling and picking purple polish off her thumbnail.

The Complete Works of Emily Dickinson lay on Mr. Jupiter's desk. It seemed to glitter in the sunlight.

Jackie didn't raise her hand either. Instead, she mumbled to herself while Bernadette recited Karla Kuskin's "Me" (fourteen lines); Emberly recited Kenn

Nesbitt's "The Amusement Park" (eight lines); and Lenny recited Ogden Nash's "The Eel" (two lines).

"Anyone else?" asked Mr. Jupiter.

Everyone looked at Jackie.

She looked down at the poem on her desk.

"Then it's time to declare the winner in our class poetry contest," said Mr. Jupiter. He moved toward the prize book.

Lil moved to stand.

And Jackie gulped. It was now or never.

"Mr. Jupiter," she said, "I have a poem."

"Humph," snorted Lil. "It'll have to be a really long one to beat me."

"It is," said Jackie. "It's 'Casey at the Bat' by Ernest L. Thayer."

For the first time in two weeks, Lil looked worried. "But that's fifty-eight lines long," she gasped. She glanced at her poetry thermometer. If Jackie really had memorized that poem, she'd win! Lil shook her head. "It's too long. You'll never remember it all."

Jackie began:

> *"The outlook wasn't brilliant for the Mudville nine that day;*

The score stood four to two, with but one inning more to play. . . ."

For the next fifteen minutes, Jackie recited and recited and recited . . . one line at a time. It was as nerve-wracking as playing in the tetherball championships. As exhausting as running a marathon. And just as exhilarating.

Jackie sprinted toward the finish line:

"And somewhere men are laughing, and somewhere children shout;
But there is no joy in Mudville—"

She took a last, deep breath.

"—mighty Casey has struck out."

For a moment the room fell silent; then—

"Home run!" whooped Calvin.

"Grand slam!" cried Rose.

"The winner and still class champion . . . ," shouted Emberly, "Jackie Jumpbaugh!"

Everyone but Lil cheered as Mr. Jupiter presented Jackie with the book. Lil blinked back a tear.

Jackie noticed. "Here," she said, holding out *The Complete Works of Emily Dickinson.* "You take it."

"Really?" said Lil. Her eyes shone. "You want *me* to have it?"

"Well, *I* don't want it," replied Jackie. "It's a book of *poetry,* for gosh sake."

Lil pressed the book to her chest for a few seconds, then waxed poetic:

> *"She tackled a ballad,*
> *She shot and she scored,*
> *She rounded the bases,*
> *I'm totally floored!"*

Jackie blushed.

And Ham smacked his lips. "Enough with the poetry, huh? When do we order pizza?"

MORAL: Slow and steady wins the race.

THE BAD, THE BEAUTIFUL, AND THE STINKY

VICTORIA SOVAINE WAS THE MOST beautiful girl in Mr. Jupiter's class . . . at least *she* thought so.

"I have the silkiest hair," she often said. "The bluest eyes. The most dazzling smile. Why, I'd be Miss America if I wasn't in the fourth grade."

Yes, Victoria had good looks. But she also had . . . a bad temper. When angry, she threw tantrums, hurled insults, screamed, kicked, and spat.

"She erupts like a volcano," said Missy.

"And then she's not so lava-ly," joked Lenny.

One morning, Mr. Jupiter clapped his hands. "Class," he said, "a skunk has forced the fifth graders to evacuate their classroom. Since they will be attending school at Mooseheart Lodge 186 until their room has been fumigated, we have been asked to take over their safety patrol positions." He picked up a sheet of paper. "I have a list of jobs. If you would like to volunteer for one, please raise your hand."

Mr. Jupiter read the list.

"I'll take playground duty," said Rose.

"I'll take hallway duty," said Stanford.

"But who wants bathroom doody?" snickered Lenny.

Mr. Jupiter shot him a warning look, then continued with the list.

Soon everyone but Victoria had volunteered for a job.

"What would you like to do, Victoria?" asked Mr. Jupiter. "Would you like to be a crossing guard? You could stop traffic."

"I certainly could," Victoria replied. "But the wind would muss my hair." She flipped a carefully curled lock over her shoulder.

"Then perhaps you would like to help in the lunchroom," suggested Mr. Jupiter. "That's an inside job."

Victoria cringed. "And scrape trays? I'd ruin my manicure." She blew on her perfectly sculpted nails, then buffed them on the sleeve of her blue satin blouse.

"Perhaps," said Mr. Jupiter, "you would like to be the kindergarten monitor. The little ones line up inside, where the wind won't blow your hair. And since there aren't any lunch trays to scrape, your nails will remain impeccable. What do you say?"

"Will I get to wear one of those orange safety patrol

vests?" she asked. "Orange sets off the highlights in my hair."

Mr. Jupiter thought a moment. "Those vests are usually reserved for the crossing guards, but I suppose we can arrange something."

"Then I'll do it," said Victoria.

By the end of her first week, Victoria knew kindergarten patrol had been the right choice. Not only were the kindergartners easy to boss, but they showered her with tokens of their affection—animal crackers, crayon drawings, fistfuls of dandelions.

Even better, they complimented her all the time.

"I like your skirt," one of them would say with a shy smile.

Or "I think you're nice."

Or—best of all—"You're so pretty."

Then Victoria would bend down so the adoring tots could give her a hug—a quick one that wouldn't wrinkle her outfit.

"Kindergartners," Victoria told Bernadette, "are very honest."

One day, Victoria hurried to kindergarten patrol. She was wearing a pair of sparkly new unicorn earrings that complemented her creamy complexion and brightened her eyes.

But when she leaned down so the little ones could get a better look, Mikey pinched his nose.

"Ick!" he squealed. "Your breath is stinky. Stinky like my dog, Moe's. He licks his butt."

"Butt breath," giggled Emily, who was in line behind him. "Victoria's got butt breath."

"Butt breath," the other kindergartners repeated like parrots. "Butt breath! Butt breath!"

Victoria felt herself steaming. . . .

"Butt breath!"

Boiling. . . .

"Butt breath!"

The bell rang.

Victoria stormed down the hall and into the school office.

"Is my breath bad?" she demanded. She huffed a big puff at Mrs. Struggles. "HAAAA!"

The principal staggered backward, knocking into a parent volunteer carrying a tray of cupcakes. Chocolate sprinkles flew everywhere.

"Your breath is so bad it deserves five days' detention," gasped Mrs. Struggles.

Victoria clenched her fists. "No, it's not! It's not!" she yelled.

She raged into the nurse's office.

"Is my breath bad?" she demanded. She huffed a big huff at Nurse Betadine. "HAAAA!"

Nurse Betadine squashed a surgical mask over her nose. "That's sick!" she gagged. "You should go home for the day. Let me call your mother."

Victoria raised her fists above her head. "Why won't anyone tell me the truth?" she shrieked.

She roared into the library.

"Is my breath bad?" she demanded. She huffed a big puff at Miss Turner. "HAAAA!"

The mascara on Miss Turner's false eyelashes melted, and her hair uncurled. "Your breath is not pretty," she croaked.

"Not pretty?" screamed Victoria. "Me? Not pretty?"

She pounded the air with her fists, stomped her feet, and hurled herself down the hall and into the fourth-grade classroom.

"She's blown her top!" shouted Amisha as Victoria banged doors and kicked over chairs.

"Victoria," Mr. Jupiter said firmly. "Stop this behavior at once."

But Victoria couldn't stop. Whirling like a blond tornado, she ripped the book reports off the bulletin board and flung them to the ground.

Calvin began chewing the eraser off his pencil.

Lil began reciting a poem about death.

And Ham ducked behind the desks and tried to crawl away.

Like a snake, Victoria whipped around. She grabbed him by his collar.

Fear filled Ham's eyes as Victoria pulled him closer and closer until their noses touched.

"Tell me the truth," she hissed. "Do I have bad breath?"

"HAAAAA!"

Ham's mouth puckered. His stomach lurched. "Y . . . y . . . yes," he stammered.

"Why is everyone lying!" shrieked Victoria. Pushing Ham away, she advanced on her classmates.

They quickly huddled behind Mr. Jupiter.

"Victoria," the teacher said calmly, "you need to control yourself. Let me teach you a few relaxation techniques I learned while cat-sitting for the Dalai Lama."

But Victoria was beyond control. Her maniacally

glittering eyes alighted on Lenny. With measured steps, she approached.

Lenny gulped. If there was ever a time for quick thinking, this was it.

She stopped in front of him. "You tell me," she snarled.

Lenny looked frantically around. What could he do?

"HAAAAA!"

He had to save himself . . .

"HAAAAAAAA!"

. . . before her bad breath knocked him unconscious.

"HAAAAAAAAAAAAAAA!"

His survival instinct kicked in.

And Lenny gave a dry little cough and dramatically cleared his throat. "Gee, Victoria," he said in a fake croaking voice, "I've got such a bad cold, I can't smell a thing."

The others pretended to sneeze, wheeze, and sniffle too.

"It looks like we've *all* caught a cold," announced Stanford.

Victoria's eyes narrowed.

But before she could erupt again, Mr. Jupiter said,

"That's not a problem. It just so happens I know the cure for the common cold. An ancient shaman told it to me while we were rafting up the Ganges River. Can you guess what it is?"

The children shook their heads.

"Spearmint!" cried Mr. Jupiter. He flipped open a tin of breath mints.

"Oooh," squealed Ham. "Goody."

He pushed his way toward the teacher, but Mr. Jupiter stopped him. "I think Victoria should have the first mint. After all, we don't want her to catch a cold like the rest of us." He turned to the still-glowering Victoria. "Have one," he urged. "On second thought . . . have two."

MORAL: In times of dire need, clever thinking is the key.

DEWEY OR DON'T WE?

MR. JUPITER'S STUDENTS LOVED THEIR Thursday-morning library visits. They checked out books, listened to stories on tape, and learned about—

"The Dewey decimal system!" gushed Miss Turner. "Not only is it an ingenious way of organizing *all* human knowledge, but it's fun, too!"

Lenny Wittier and Bruce Vanderbanter, however, had another reason for loving library time— *INTERNATIONAL GEOGRAPHIC!*

Plucking the latest issue from the magazine rack, they huddled in the Easy-to-Read section and pored over its pages.

Thrilling!

Titillating!

Downright naughty!

The boys had discovered the magazine last year. For weeks they had hidden behind bookshelves and tittered over photographs of Tahitian men in grass skirts, tattooed dogs, and Bavarian dooglehorns. Too soon, however, the school year—and their magazine time—had ended. Impatiently, the boys had waited for fall and the new issues.

Now they turned to a photograph of topless tribal women.

Lenny snickered.

Bruce giggled.

Miss Turner cleared her throat. "What are you boys doing back here?"

Lenny tried to cover the picture with his arm. "N-nothing," he stammered.

"Yeah," added Bruce. "Nothing."

Miss Turner put out her hand.

The boys couldn't help noticing the magenta polish on her well-sculpted nails. They glanced at each other. Since when did Miss Turner do her nails?

"Hand me that magazine," said the librarian.

Reluctantly, Lenny surrendered it.

Miss Turner looked from the photograph to the red-faced boys. She rolled her eyes. "If you two aren't old enough to appreciate the infinite beauty of our world and its varied cultures, then you're not old enough to read this magazine."

"But we weren't reading it," said Lenny.

"We were just looking at the pictures," said Bruce.

Miss Turner bit her lip and put on her stern librarian's face. "Now come and join the rest of the class in the reading nook. We're having our lesson on the Dewey decimal system."

For the next fifteen minutes, Miss Turner chirped and bubbled about the Dewey decimal system. "The system was invented by the brilliant librarian Melvil Dewey. It is based on ten broad categories, such as 100 to 199, Philosophy and Psychology; 200 to 299, Religion; 300 to 399, Social Sciences; and so on. Each broad category divides into nine subcategories spanning a range from ten to ninety. Each subcategory is further divided into nine specialized topics ranging from one to nine. Decimals are added to break the topics down even further. Isn't that fascinating?"

The children yawned.

"But don't take my word for it," she continued. "Take *theirs*."

Up popped a hand puppet wearing flowered bathing trunks and carrying a surfboard. "Cowabunga, dudes," said the puppet in a voice that sounded very much like Mr. Jupiter's.

The children blinked.

A second puppet appeared. This one had sharp teeth and a fin attached to its back. It slunk toward the surfer puppet.

"I'm in trouble, dudes!" cried the surfer puppet. "Quick, tell me what tool I would use to find information on repelling a shark?"

None of the children answered.

"Tell me!" the surfer puppet shouted as the shark swam closer.

Still nobody answered.

"Please!" screamed the surfer puppet.

"Um," Bernadette finally said, "the Dewey decimal system?"

"You're right, dudette!" cried the surfer puppet. "But—" The shark pounced. "You're too late. ARGH!"

The puppets wrestled their way out of sight.

The children clapped.

Then two new puppets popped up. One was a little old lady with a big nose. The other was a little old man with a bigger nose.

"Oh, Puh-uunch!" cried the little old lady.

"Yes, Judy?" answered the little old man.

"I have a surprise for you," said Judy.

"Then give it to me," said Punch.

WHACK!

Judy smacked Punch over the head with a broom.

"Ouch!" shouted Punch. He turned to the children. "It looks as if I need to learn about head injuries. How can I find the information?"

"The school nurse?" suggested Amisha.

"The Internet?" suggested Ashley Z.

"I know! I know!" cried Missy. "The Dewey decimal system. You'd use the Dewey decimal system."

"Hooray!" exclaimed Punch. "I'm saved!"

"That's what you think," screeched Judy. She chased Punch offstage.

The children clapped and laughed as a penguin puppet popped up.

"What tool would I use to find information about refrigeration?" it asked.

"The Dewey decimal system!" the children cried.

Now a Benjamin Franklin puppet popped up. "What can help me find books about electricity?"

"The Dewey decimal system!" the children cried again.

Now a sumo wrestler puppet popped up. "What system can help me find books about diaper rash?"

"The Dewey decimal system!" the children cried yet again.

Then Miss Turner and all the puppets burst into song:

> *"Numbers, numbers in a row.*
> *Tell us where nonfiction goes."*

The children joined in:

> *"Gives us facts and gives us rules.*
> *The Dewey decimal system's cool."*

With each verse, they grew louder and more enthusiastic, until everyone was clapping and laughing and cheering for the Dewey decimal system.

Everyone, that is, except Lenny and Bruce.

"I don't get it," whispered Lenny.

"Me either," Bruce whispered back.

"Shhhh!" hissed Stanford. "I can't hear what she's saying."

Miss Turner looked toward Lenny and Bruce. "Join the fun!" she urged them.

But the boys didn't think the Dewey decimal system

was all that fun, not even when Miss Turner cried, "Do you know about the Dewey decimal system?" and everyone replied, "Do we? Dewey? Boy, do we!"

"That was the best library lesson ever," Stanford declared minutes later as the fourth graders lined up to head back to class.

Lenny pretended to gag.

Bruce pretended to choke.

And Miss Turner sighed.

She turned to Mr. Jupiter and, for the first time since meeting him, forgot to bat her eyelashes. "I wish I could find some way to spark those two's interest. I wish I could turn them into Dewey whizzes."

Mr. Jupiter nodded. "When I worked at Transylvania Elementary I had the same problem with the son of a local count. The boy just couldn't sink his teeth into the subject." He patted her hand, and the librarian almost swooned. "I'm sure you'll think of something."

The following Thursday, Lenny and Bruce headed straight for the magazine rack. But the *International Geographic*s were—

"Gone!" gasped Lenny.

"Yes," said Miss Turner. "I've hidden them."

"Hidden?" said Bruce.

"Actually," explained Miss Turner, "I've shelved them using the Dewey decimal system."

"Huh?" grunted the boys.

"Ordinarily, I wouldn't shelve books and magazines together," continued Miss Turner, "but in order to show you how wonderfully versatile the system is, I've taken a few liberties."

"Huh?" the boys grunted again.

"You see," Miss Turner went on, "I've matched information on the inside of the magazine with its corresponding Dewey decimal number, thus finding the perfect place for them on the bookshelves. If you want to read them, you'll have to find them." Pivoting on the heels of her strappy sandals, she sashayed away. Only the scent of her new perfume lingered.

Bruce sighed with disappointment. "I guess I'm back to reading books."

"Not so fast," said Lenny. "I'm not about to be beaten by a librarian."

He trolled up and down the aisles of bookshelves, his eyes flicking right and left.

For the first time ever, he noticed the numbers on

the spines of each book. He noticed the corresponding numbers on the end of each of the bookshelves.

"Are those Dewey decimal numbers?" he asked Bruce.

"I think so," said Bruce.

"Huh," said Lenny. "I'm beginning to see the connection." He swept past books about space and time (Dewey decimal numbers 114 and 115),

past books about religion (Dewey decimal number 200),

past books about criminal law (345) and railroad transportation (385) and—

Aha!

There, wedged in with books about customs, etiquette, and folklore (390), was a stack of *International Geographic*s.

"I get it," said Bruce. "Some of the magazine articles are about life in other countries. You know, their special customs."

"Clever of her," said Lenny. "But not clever enough."

The two crept behind the new books section and opened a magazine to an article about Bikini Island.

From across the room, Miss Turner watched . . . and smiled.

* * *

The next Thursday, Lenny and Bruce dashed to 390, but—

"They've been reshelved," said Miss Turner.

The boys groaned.

"Isn't the Dewey decimal system wonderful?" chirped the librarian. "It's so flexible."

"And so confusing," groaned Lenny.

"Not really," replied Miss Turner. "Not if you have a chart." She pointed to a poster on the wall. On it was listed the entire Dewey decimal system.

The boys studied it a moment. Then they started searching. . . .

Languages of East and Southeast Asia (495).

Gas Mechanics (533).

Microbiology (576).

"Where can they be?" wailed Lenny.

"How about Zoology?" suggested Bruce. "Those magazines have lots of articles about animals in them."

"Good idea," said Lenny. "What's the decimal number for zoology?"

"591," said Stanford, who was walking past.

The boys made a beeline for the bookshelf, then

spent the rest of their library time giggling behind Biographies.

The next Thursday, Bruce pulled a piece of paper out of his pocket. They knew Miss Turner would have reshelved the *International Geographic*s, and they were ready. Earlier they had made a list of categories the magazine might be shelved under. Now they split up.

Lenny headed for Birds (598).

Nothing.

Bruce dashed toward Human Anatomy (611).

Nada.

Lenny found his way to Agriculture (630).

Zip.

"Where can they be?" asked Bruce when they'd crossed the last topic off their list. He sighed in defeat.

That was when Miss Turner appeared. "Did you boys read that article about the Taj Mahal?" she asked. "It was absolutely fascinating!"

Lenny looked at Bruce.

Bruce looked at Lenny.

"That's it!" they cried in unison.

They found the magazines shelved under Buildings (690).

Victoriously, they pulled the magazines down just as Mr. Jupiter clapped his hands. "Everyone line up."

"Rotten luck," growled Lenny. He put the magazines back.

The following Thursday, Miss Turner had a surprise for the fourth graders. "Instead of checking out books," she said, "we're going to play the Dewey decimal game. The winner will receive a special prize."

Miss Turner explained the rules. Each student would be asked a question about the Dewey decimal system. If the student answered correctly, he would remain standing. If the student answered incorrectly, she would be asked to sit down. The last student left standing would be the winner.

Stanford turned to Lenny and Bruce. "I bet you wish you'd paid closer attention now," he said.

Lenny shrugged. Who needed to pay attention when he could use the chart? He glanced toward it, and his heart sank. Miss Turner had taken the poster down!

Bruce had noticed too. "We're going to be the first kids out," he groaned.

The boys dragged themselves to their feet as Miss Turner shuffled through a stack of index cards and read the first question. "Under what number would you find a book about tetherball. Jackie?"

Jackie didn't hesitate. "796," she answered.

"Correct," said Miss Turner.

"Woo-woo-woo!" whooped Calvin and Humphrey. They pumped their fists in the air.

"Rachel," said Miss Turner, "this question is for you. A book about public speaking can be found under what number?"

"Pffft," Rachel said.

"No, I'm sorry," said Miss Turner. "The number is 791."

"Woo-woo-woo!" whooped Calvin and Humphrey again.

Miss Turner turned to Lenny.

Beads of sweat broke out on his forehead.

"Tell me," said Miss Turner, "under what number would you find a book about customs, etiquette, and folklore?"

Lenny couldn't believe his luck. She'd asked him something he knew! "390," he said with confidence. "The answer is 390."

Miss Turner nodded and smiled, then looked at Bruce. "Books about zoology can be found where?"

"591!" shouted Bruce.

"Correct," said Miss Turner. "And I like your enthusiasm." She smiled at Mr. Jupiter.

He smiled back.

And so the game went. Question after question. Answer after answer. Student after student after student.

Ashlee A., Ashleigh B., and Ashley Z. went down in the second round. But not Lenny or Bruce.

Jackie went down in the fourth round. But not Lenny or Bruce.

Amisha, Missy, Victoria, and Lil all went down in the sixth round. But not Lenny or Bruce.

By the tenth round only Stanford, Lenny, and Bruce remained standing.

"Stanford," said Miss Turner, "where would I find a book about buildings?"

Stanford shot the other two a triumphant look before answering, "328."

"No, I'm sorry, that's incorrect," said Miss Turner. "Does either of you boys know?"

"690!" they cried in unison.

Miss Turner grinned. "I declare this contest a tie," she said. "And now for your prize." She reached behind her desk and pulled out a stack of . . .

119

"*International Geographic*s!" whooped Bruce.

"Geography and travel, 910," added Lenny.

Then together the boys cried, "Do we know about the Dewey decimal system? Do we? Dewey? Boy, do we!"

MORAL: Necessity is the mother of invention.

HAM AND BEANS

ONE MONDAY MORNING, MRS. GROS-
singer visited the fourth grade. She smiled at the children with her big white teeth. "As president of your
PTO, I'm pleased to announce that your class has
won the schoolwide Bean Around the World geography
contest."

"Geography contest?" repeated Humphrey. "What
geography contest? I don't remember entering any geography contest."

Mrs. Grossinger held up a worksheet bordered with
pictures of grinning globes and dancing lima beans.
"Remember this?" she said.

The children looked puzzled.

Then Calvin said, "Wait! You mean we won *that*
contest?"

Mrs. Grossinger nodded.

The children looked even more puzzled.

Weeks ago the PTO president had delivered that
very same piece of paper to their classroom. "As part
of the contest," she had explained, "you will be

expected to work together as a class using encyclopedias, atlases, and other sources to answer the questions on this worksheet."

But the fourth graders hadn't taken the contest seriously.

"Who wants to bother with an atlas?" Lenny had asked.

No one did—not even Stanford. "I'm much too busy studying for next month's juggling test to bother with some ridiculous contest," he had said.

So instead of looking up the answers, the fourth graders had made them up.

This is what they had turned in:

AESOP ELEMENTARY PTO PRESENTS:
BEAN AROUND THE WORLD GEOGRAPHY CONTEST
Please research and carefully answer the following:
1. What is the most slippery country?
Greece.
2. What language do they speak in Cuba?
Cubic.
3. What type of birds are found in Portugal?
Portu-geese.

4. Where is the English Channel?

Between the Spanish and the French Channels.

5. Name three famous poles.

North, South, and Tad.

6. What are the Great Plains?

The Concorde, the stealth fighter, and the 747.

7. Why is the Mississippi River so unusual?

Because it has four *i*'s but can't see.

8. What is the fastest country?

Russia, because the people are always Russian.

9. Why is Alabama the smartest state in the USA?

Because it has four As and one B.

10. What is the capital of South Dakota?

Pierre.

Now Mrs. Grossinger managed to smile even bigger. "Congratulations," she said. "You got the most answers right."

Lenny waggled his eyebrows. "How could that have *bean*?"

"*Beans* me," Bruce said.

"Does this mean we're superior *beans*?" Missy said.

Mrs. Grossinger's smile turned frosty.

"I'm *bean*-wildered," Jackie said.

"I've never *bean* so confused," Victoria said.

"To *bean* or nacho to *bean*," Lil said. "That is the *queso*."

Mrs. Grossinger stopped smiling entirely. Thumping a jar onto Mr. Jupiter's desk—right between his walrus tusk and his Lunganga pig mask— she snapped, "Here's your prize," and stomped toward the door.

"*Bean* nice seeing you!" Bernadette called after her.

The door slammed.

The children looked at their prize.

"Jelly beans!" exclaimed Ham Samitch from the very last seat in the very last row. "I love, love, love jelly beans! Can we eat them now, Mr. Jupiter? Can we? Huh?"

Mr. Jupiter nodded. "Each of you may come up and reach into the jar," he said. "We'll start with the very first person in the very first row."

Ham raised his hand. "Mr. Jupiter," he whined, "do we have to go front to back? Can't we go back to front? Just this once?"

Mr. Jupiter shook his head. "No, Ham, we can't."

"But I'll get my candy last," Ham whined again.

"Did you know," replied Mr. Jupiter, "that in the

Indonesian province of Budong-Budong, where I once raised Komodo dragons, it is considered an honor to be last?"

"But what if there aren't any jelly beans left by the time I get my turn?" Ham was whimpering now. "What if there aren't enough?"

"There's plenty for everyone," said Mr. Jupiter.

Ham wasn't so sure. Nervously, he watched Bernadette go first. Reaching into the jar, she pulled out eight jelly beans—three pink, two yellow, two purple, and a green.

"That's too many," he howled. "Too many!"

Rachel went second. Shyly, she reached into the jar and picked out two orange beans.

"Not the orange ones," Ham sobbed. "Orange is my favorite color."

Lil was third. Before helping herself to one green, two yellow, and three purple beans, she took a deep breath and waxed poetic:

> "A jar full of jelly beans,
> So colorful and sweet,
> As lovely as a painting,
> And a very tasty treat."

"Hurry up, huh?" Ham groaned. He wiped the drool from his lips.

One by one the fourth graders dipped their hands into the jar.

One by one they pulled out four jelly beans . . . eight jelly beans . . . fourteen jelly beans.

"Save some for me!" Ham cried again and again. "Save some for me."

Finally, it was his turn. Hurrying up the aisle to Mr. Jupiter's desk, he thrust his pudgy hand into the jar and clutched as many as his fist could hold—fourteen green, ten red, six orange, four yellow, and three black.

"I got more than anyone else," he crowed.

But when he tried to pull out his bulging fist, it was—

"Stuck!" he wailed. "I'm stuck."

"Oh, dear," said Mr. Jupiter. "That is a problem."

Ham tugged and twisted. He pushed and pulled. He even tried tapping the jar on the edge of the desk the way his mother did when she couldn't get the mayonnaise open.

Nothing worked.

"I want my jelly beans!" wailed Ham.

"Try using your head," suggested Mr. Jupiter.

Ham did.

Thump!

"Ouch!"

He was still stuck.

"Call Mr. Swill!" cried the boy. "He'll know what to do."

So Mr. Jupiter pressed the intercom button.

ZZZ-CRACK!

"Send Mr. Swill on the double," said Mr. Jupiter.

"Roger that," replied Mrs. Shorthand.

Minutes later, the janitor arrived. He tapped the jar with his screwdriver and mopped around the area.

But Ham was still stuck.

"Call Nurse Betadine!" he cried. "She'll know what to do."

ZZZ-CRACK!

Nurse Betadine strode into the classroom. She took Ham's temperature and slapped a Band-Aid on the jar.

But he was still stuck.

"Call Miss Turner!" cried Ham. "She'll know what to do."

ZZZ-CRACK!

Miss Turner sashayed into the classroom. She spritzed the jar with perfume ("Love's Life Scentence," said Victoria with an approving sniff) and read a chapter from *The Life of Melvil Dewey.*

But Ham was still stuck.

A tear trickled down his plump cheek.

"Life is so unfair," he moaned. "I waited so long to get my hands on these jelly beans, and now . . ." He gave a breathy sob. "Now I'll never get to taste them."

He watched, mouth watering, as Amisha popped a pink bean into her mouth. "Mmm, mmm, good."

Emberly munched on a yellow one. "Yummy."

Rachel licked an orange one. "Pffft."

Ham gave another little sob. Then, from desperation, an idea grew.

What if I dropped some jelly beans? he wondered. *Just a few . . . just enough to pull my hand out?*

Slowly, carefully, he opened his fingers. Three green beans rolled back into the jar.

"That should be enough," he muttered.

But his hand was still stuck.

He opened his fingers a little wider. Six orange beans fell back into the jar.

"Not the orange ones," he moaned. "They're my favorite."

But his hand was still stuck.

He opened his fingers a little bit wider still.

Out fell seven green, eight red, and three yellow beans.

And out came his hand.

"I'm free!" whooped Ham.

Even better, in his palm he still held four green, two red, one yellow, and three black beans—half a handful. Popping them into his mouth, he chewed, swallowed, sighed. "Delicious."

Then he looked longingly back at the jar. "Can we have seconds, Mr. Jupiter? Can we? Huh?"

"Don't *bean* ridiculous," replied Mr. Jupiter.

MORAL: Half a handful is better than none.

MISSY'S LOST MITTENS

MR. JUPITER'S CLASS WAS BUNDLING UP for recess—parkas, snow boots, hats, and scarves.

Missy Place slipped on her zebra-striped jacket, then reached into her pocket for her black knitted mittens. She pulled out—

—a wad of used tissue and a lint-covered Life Saver.

"Oh, no!" gasped Missy. "Not again." Dropping to her knees, she searched everywhere—inside the Polynesian ceremonial slit drums, under the stuffed giant sloth, behind the brass astrolabe, on top of the piranha tank, and even in the shrunken head collection. But it was no use.

"I've lost my mittens," she wailed.

"Big deal," said Victoria, shrugging. "After all, they weren't special mittens, not like *mine.*" Victoria held up a hot-pink fur-lined pair. "Nobody's mittens are as special as *my* mittens."

"But they're the thirty-seventh pair I've lost this week," sniffled Missy.

"I guess that makes you a real loser," said Victoria.

"Go away, Victoria," said Rose. She patted Missy's arm. "It'll be okay."

"No, it won't," moaned Missy. "My mom said if I lost another pair she was going to diaper-pin them to my sleeves like she does for Davie." Davie was Missy's little brother. He was in preschool.

Just then, Mr. Jupiter appeared. "Is there a problem, girls?"

"Missy's lost her mittens," said Rose.

"Again," sighed Missy. She wiped her nose on her sleeve.

"Have you looked in the ceremonial slit drums?" asked Mr. Jupiter.

Missy nodded.

"And under the sloth?"

Missy nodded again.

"And behind the astrolabe, on top of the piranha tank, and even in the shrunken heads?"

Missy sobbed, "I've looked everywhere."

"Then there is only one place left," said Mr. Jupiter. "Lost and Found."

"*Lost and Found?*" shrieked Missy. "I can't go to Lost and Found. I'll get lost and I'll never get found."

"Nonsense," said Mr. Jupiter.

"It's true," said Rose.

Located in the school's basement, Lost and Found was a graveyard of lunch boxes and Windbreakers, umbrellas and spelling books, colored pencils and macaroni art projects. The place was so dark, so big, so creepy that Aesop's students stayed away from it the way fourth-grade boys stayed away from a Girl Scout meeting. And what happened to the kid who naively wandered into Lost and Found in search of his baseball mitt? No one knew for sure. But rumor had it that the skeleton hanging in the art/science room had once been a bright, happy, normal kid who'd had the misfortune of blundering into Lost and Found.

Now Missy begged, "You have to come with me, Mr. Jupiter. You have to!"

"Of course," he replied.

After sending the rest of the class out to recess, Mr. Jupiter pulled a headlamp from his desk—"Left over from my spelunking days," he explained—and strapped it onto his pith helmet.

Minutes later the two stood at the edge of Lost and Found's vast, inky blackness. The light from Mr. Jupiter's headgear barely pierced its gloom.

Missy's heart pounded and she clutched Mr.

Jupiter's arm. "I don't need my mittens," she croaked. "Really, Mr. Jupiter. Let's go back."

But Mr. Jupiter just patted her white-knuckled hand. "Nonsense," he said. "You must have your mittens or your fingers will freeze." He stepped into the darkness that was Lost and Found, spelunked to the room's center, and pulled on an overhead chain. The room filled with light.

Missy gasped.

The place looked magical—almost like Aladdin's cave. Instead of heaps of gold and mountains of jewels, however, there were heaps of snow boots and mountains of bean bag animals.

And there wasn't a skeleton in sight.

Missy's fears vanished.

"Let's get started," said Mr. Jupiter, switching off his headlamp. "What do your mittens look like?"

Missy shrugged. "You know—the usual."

Mr. Jupiter nodded and began digging through a nearby pile while Missy pawed through a box.

She found a paperback copy of *Mr. Popper's Penguins,* a headless Barbie doll, and a pair of swim fins.

"Are these your mittens?" Mr. Jupiter suddenly cried. He held up a knitted gold pair covered in flashing pink sequins and shiny blue bows. When he tugged the left thumb, the mittens sang "Twinkle, Twinkle, Little Star."

Missy was enchanted by them. They were special, even more special than Victoria's. How she wished they belonged to her, but . . . "Mine aren't as nice as those," she confessed.

She and Mr. Jupiter went back to digging.

A dirty sock. Half a baloney sandwich. A cuckoo clock.

"Are these your mittens?" Mr. Jupiter asked a few minutes later. He held up a fuzzy pink pair that looked like two pink pigs. The pig mittens had eyes, ears, and a snout that oinked when Mr. Jupiter squeezed it.

Missy adored them. She desperately wished they were hers, but . . . "Those aren't mine either," she admitted. "Mine are black and knit and very, very boring."

They dug some more.

A pencil case. A stringless yo-yo. A triceratops tooth.

"I wondered where that had disappeared to," said Mr. Jupiter. He pocketed the tooth and kept digging. Soon he held up a plain black knitted pair. "Are these your mittens?" he asked.

Missy clapped her hands in delight. "You found them, Mr. Jupiter. Thank you!" She slipped them on.

"Perhaps," said Mr. Jupiter with a smile, "you should have a few extra pairs in case you lose those again." He held out the musical mittens and the pig mittens.

"But don't those belong to someone else?" she asked.

"Believe me," said Mr. Jupiter, "your honesty has made you the true owner of these mittens."

Missy grinned, then eagerly stripped off her old pair and slipped on the musical ones. After tucking the others carefully into her coat pocket, she raced out to recess.

On the playground, Missy was the center of attention.

"Did you find any ghosts down there?" asked Humphrey.

"Any skeletons?" asked Lenny.

"Any trolls?" asked Calvin.

"Nope," replied Missy. "But I did find these." She held up her hands so that everyone could admire her new mittens.

"They're so special," said Amisha, touching the bright sequins.

Victoria's eyes narrowed.

"Really special," said Lil, tying one of the bows.

Victoria's nostrils flared.

"The most special mittens I've ever seen," said Rose. She hummed along with "Twinkle, Twinkle."

Victoria ground her teeth and turned pea green.

The next morning just before recess, Victoria hid her hot-pink fur-lined mittens in the trash can.

"Mr. Jupiter," she said with a little sob, "I've lost my mittens."

Mr. Jupiter raised his eyebrows. "Indeed?" he said. "Then we'd better check Lost and Found."

Smirking, Victoria followed Mr. Jupiter to the basement.

Mr. Jupiter began digging.

Victoria watched. She tapped her foot impatiently.

A few minutes later, Mr. Jupiter held up a glorious pair. Made of sleek white fur and trimmed in gold and pearls, they played Beethoven's Fifth Symphony when the teacher shook them.

"Are these the mittens you lost, Victoria?" asked Mr. Jupiter. He watched her closely.

"Oh, yes!" trilled Victoria. "Yes." Eagerly, she reached for the mittens.

"There they are," cooed a voice from the doorway.

Victoria turned to see—

Was it?

Could it be?

It was!

It was Miss Turner looking—Victoria shook her head in disbelief—almost glamorous in a white fur coat trimmed in gold braid and seed pearls.

"You've found my mittens, you naughty kittens," the librarian purred. She held out a bare hand to Mr. Jupiter. "Would you help me put them on?"

"Of course," said Mr. Jupiter. He slipped first the right mitten and then the left onto Miss Turner's hands. Like Cinderella's slippers, they were a perfect fit.

"But . . . but . . . what about me?" wailed Victoria. "I don't have any mittens."

"How unfortunate," said Mr. Jupiter. "I guess you'll have to keep your hands in your pockets."

Gnashing her teeth, Victoria huffed back up the stairs. But before going out to recess, she reached into the trash can for her old hot-pink pair.

"Oh, no!'" she wailed. "Mr. Swill emptied the trash!"

MORAL: Honesty is the best policy.

STICKS AND STONES

IT WAS VALENTINE'S DAY, AND MR. Jupiter's students were opening their cards.

Emberly opened one with a lollipop taped to it:

I'M A SUCKER FOR YOU!

He smiled across the room at Ham.

Jackie opened one with Cupid wearing a baseball glove.

HAPPY VALENTINE'S DAY FROM A REAL GLOVER BOY!

She high-fived Humphrey.

Bernadette opened an all-black one.

I SEE YOUR FACE WHILE I AM DREAMING,

THAT'S WHY I ALWAYS WAKE UP SCREAMING!

She stuck out her tongue at Lenny.

Then Miss Turner pushed open the door. A blond vision in tight-fitting pink, she panted, "Don't mind me," as she struggled up the aisle toward Mr. Jupiter. "I've just got a little treat for your teacher."

She dropped a heart-shaped box of chocolates, a big pink teddy bear, two dozen red roses, and a bouquet of helium-filled balloons that read BE MINE onto his desk. "Happy Valentine's Day," she said between gasps for breath.

Mr. Jupiter smiled. "Thank you, Paige," he said. "I have something for you, too." He handed her—

"A stick?" said Miss Turner.

Mr. Jupiter nodded. "From the Polynesian commona-wanna-hugga-ya shrub. In Fiji this stick is a gift—a gift given only to good friends."

"Good friends?" repeated Miss Turner. She blinked back a tear and touched the stick tenderly.

Mr. Jupiter nodded.

And Miss Turner pressed the stick to her cheek. "I'll cherish it always," she sighed. She floated out the door.

"I have something for each of you, too," Mr. Jupiter said to the children after the librarian had left. He gave each of them—

"A rock?" said Calvin.

"Not a rock," corrected Mr. Jupiter. "A pooka stone."

"Huh?" said Ham.

"To the Baluba tribe of Hubba Island, the pooka

stone is a symbol of deep affection," explained Mr. Jupiter.

Suddenly red-cheeked, the children stared at him.

"I picked them up along the beach while visiting their chief over the holidays," added Mr. Jupiter.

The children kept staring at him.

"Don't you like them?" asked Mr. Jupiter.

Missy raised her hand. "Does this mean that you . . . um . . . *love* us, Mr. Jupiter?"

"I care about each and every one of you," he admitted.

Embarrassed, the children wiggled in their seats.

"Gee," Rose finally said. "All we got you was this stupid valentine."

She handed him a card that read:

WE LOVE TO "B" YOUR "A" STUDENTS.

It was signed by everyone in the class.

Too choked up to speak, Mr. Jupiter placed his hand over his heart and wrestled with his emotions. At last he managed to sniffle, "I'm deeply moved by your outpouring of affection. Thank you from the bottom of my heart."

For several seconds, teacher and students smiled stupidly at one another.

Then Mr. Jupiter broke the spell. Picking up the box of candy Miss Turner had given him, he said, "Chocolate, anyone?"

Ham hurried up the aisle.

MORAL: No act of kindness—no matter how big or how small—is ever wasted.

MARCH MADNESS

MARCH WAS TESTING TIME AT AESOP Elementary School.

"Everyone take out a number two pencil," directed Mr. Jupiter.

Calvin raised his hand. "Are we being given the I.S.B.N.A.C.T.'s?" he asked.

"No, no," corrected Bernadette. "These are the Y.M.C.A.G.R.E.'s."

"Actually," said Rose, "they're the H.I.J.K.L. M.N.O.P.'s."

In the back row, Stanford snorted. "Get serious," he said. "We're taking the E.S.B.A.F.C.A.E.F.G.A.E.'s, otherwise known as the Every State Basic Abilities and Fundamental Cognitive Assessment of Essential Fourth Grade Achievement Evaluation Test."

"Whatever," shrugged the others.

"I couldn't agree more," said Mr. Jupiter. "Still . . ." He looked around the room. "Does everyone have a pencil?"

The children nodded.

"Then I suppose we should get started," he said.

And for the rest of the month, the fourth graders did nothing else.

MORAL: Time is often wasted on things of little consequence.

CATCH!

EMBERLY EVERCLASS HAD THE BEST attendance record at Aesop Elementary School. Since his first morning in kindergarten, he hadn't missed a single day—not one.

"Don't you ever get sick?" asked Rose one afternoon.

"Nope," said Emberly.

"Don't you ever go on vacation?" asked Amisha.

"Nope," said Emberly.

"Don't you ever play hooky?" asked Lenny.

"Nope," said Emberly.

But all these questions made Emberly start to think about it.

And the more he thought about it, the more he realized the truth:

He would have traded all his perfect attendance medals for just one single day off.

He could just see himself lounging on the couch in his Incredible Hunk pj's, watching cartoons, doing . . . NOTHING!

"Beautiful," he sighed.

"I know I am, but what are you?" asked Victoria.

"Absent," vowed Emberly.

The next morning before school, Emberly gave an award-winning performance. He cough-coughed. He sniff-sniffled. He pretended to wheeze as he groaned, "Ohhhhh, I'm soooooo sick."

His father wasn't fooled. "Get moving," he said. "You don't want to be late."

Besides having perfect attendance, Emberly was always punctual.

"What's a guy have to do to get a day off?" he muttered.

Minutes later, he was out the door.

A block from school, he saw Varicella Zoster and her mother playing in their front yard. The three-year-old, he noticed, was covered with red spots.

"What's wrong with Varicella?" he asked Mrs. Zoster.

"Stay back!" warned Mrs. Zoster. "Varicella's sick. She has chicken pox."

"Catch!" cried Varicella. She tossed a ball to Ham.

Emberly dodged it. "She doesn't look sick," he said. "Except for the spots."

"She doesn't feel sick, either," said Mrs. Zoster, "but the little darling can't go back to nursery school until her spots form scabs."

"No school!" chirped Varicella.

"No school?" Emberly asked curiously. "Why not?"

"Because she's highly contagious," explained Mrs. Zoster. "If Varicella went to school now, in two weeks' time the rest of her class would come down with the chicken pox."

"Two weeks!" chirped Varicella.

Mrs. Zoster nodded. "That's how long it is between the time a person is exposed to the chicken pox and the time they break out."

Emberly wondered what he would be doing in two weeks. Looking into his future, he saw the usual—book reports, spelling tests, organic geochemistry.

He seized his chance.

Swooping down, he kissed Varicella SMACK! on her red-speckled nose.

"Yuck!" yelped Varicella.

"Oh, no!" shrieked Mrs. Zoster.

"So long, perfect attendance!" whooped Emberly. And he ran the rest of the way to school.

*   *   *

During morning announcements, Mrs. Struggles said, "Just a reminder that Nurse Betadine will be administering booster shots to the fourth grade. This will happen in two weeks."

Two weeks?

Everyone but Emberly groaned.

During lunch, Mrs. Bunz bellowed through her bullhorn, "Listen up, fourth graders. You've just been picked as my new cafeteria helpers. You start in two weeks."

Two weeks?

Everyone but Emberly moaned.

And during gym class, Mrs. Gluteal said, "Guess what, boys and girls? Our next physical fitness unit will be . . . ballet! Be sure to bring a pair of tights to class in the next two weeks."

Two weeks?

Everyone but Emberly whined.

Later that day, during science, Mr. Jupiter clapped his hands. "Class, I have some exciting news."

The fourth graders turned off their Bunsen burners and pushed up their safety goggles. They waited to hear the exciting news.

"We will be taking a field trip to the Esther C.

Williams Public Natatorium, where we will conduct hands-on experiments with buoyancy and currents."

The fourth graders were still waiting for the exciting news.

"Aren't you thrilled?" asked Mr. Jupiter.

"I guess," said Calvin. He shot a confused look at Missy.

"Maybe," said Missy. Bewildered, she looked at Rachel.

"Pffft," said Rachel. She slid down in her seat.

In the front row, Stanford raised his hand. "I'm thrilled," he said.

"You're annoying," said Lenny.

"Little do you know," sniffed Stanford. "*Natatorium* is the scientific word for 'swimming pool.' Mr. Jupiter is taking us to the swimming pool to learn about floating and splashing."

"I might even teach you a few water polo moves," added Mr. Jupiter. "After all, I hold the 1996 Water Polo World Cup."

"Hooray!" cried Ashlee A.

"Whoopee!" cried Ashleigh B.

"This is going to be lots more fun than last year's

trip to the American Museum of Natural Gas!" cried Ashley Z.

"Yeah," agreed Humphrey. "That trip really stunk."

At his desk, Emberly decided this was the best day of his life—first the chicken pox and now the swimming pool!

Bernadette raised her hand. "When are we going?" she asked.

"In two weeks," replied Mr. Jupiter.

Two weeks?

Everyone but Emberly cheered.

"I'm buying a new bathing suit," said Victoria, "a blue one to match my eyes."

"I'm bringing my inflatable alligator raft," said Ham.

"I need a new nose plug," said Melvin.

The others ignored him.

"Mr. Jupiter," Emberly cried, "can we move the trip up? Can we go tomorrow, or . . . or . . . what about next month?"

Mr. Jupiter shook his head. "The details have already been worked out. Is there a problem?"

"No," replied Emberly. He slumped in his seat.

Maybe, he told himself, he wouldn't break out with chicken pox. Maybe Varicella wasn't all that contagious. But deep down, he knew the truth. In two weeks he'd be scratching and itching while his classmates splashed and swam.

His misery showed on his face.

"You look drearier than a rainy day," said Lil. And she broke into verse:

> *"Down your sad face*
> *A lone tear will trace*
> *Until it reaches the place*
> *Where unhappiness dwells."*

"Cut it out, Lil," said Emberly. "I'm not in a poetic mood."

"What's the matter?" asked Calvin. "Don't you like swimming pools?"

"I love swimming pools," said Emberly, "but . . ."

Suddenly inspiration struck.

Emberly leaped to his feet. "Friends," he said in his most persuasive voice—the one he had learned at the carnival last summer. "I have a secret to tell you."

Curious, the others gathered around.

"On the day of the field trip, I will be doing something far more wonderful than swimming. I will be lounging on my couch in my pj's, watching cartoons and doing . . . NOTHING!"

"Nothing?" said Victoria.

"Nothing," repeated Emberly. "Now, I ask you—what could be better than that? Yes, you will have the pleasure of paddling around a pool for a few brief hours. But the rest of the week while I'm lounging, you'll be getting shots, getting shouted at, and getting chapped from too-tight tights."

"Icky poo," shivered Humphrey.

"You can say that again," said Emberly.

"Icky poo," shivered Humphrey.

Emberly kept talking. "There is a way to save yourself from this misery. All you have to do is visit Varicella Zoster today—go right after school—and give the small tot a big kiss. In return, Varicella will give you a very slight case of the chicken pox. Once you've made this exchange, you, too, can stay home from school. What do you say, friends?"

"I say, 'Sign me up,'" said Bernadette.

"I say, 'Count me in,'" said Calvin.

"I say, 'Baloney!'" cried Melvin. He elbowed his way

to the front of the group. "You know what I think? I think you don't really want to get the chicken pox now. I think if there was some way you could get rid of the germs, you would. I think you really want to go swimming, but since you can't, you don't want anyone else to go either."

"Ignore him," said Emberly.

But for once, the others didn't.

MORAL: Misery loves company.

THE PROBLEM WITH BEING ERNEST

MR. JUPITER CLAPPED HIS HANDS. "Class," he said, "I would like you to meet Ernest Moomaday. He and his family just moved here from Kathmandu."

The class stared at Ernest.

Ernest stared at his feet.

"Ernest," said Mr. Jupiter, "why don't you tell us a little bit about yourself?"

Ernest didn't know what to say. His knees were shaking and his throat felt dry as chalk dust. He kept his eyes on his shoes.

"Do you have any hobbies?" Mr. Jupiter asked encouragingly.

Ernest touched his vest. He had crocheted it himself, using a lovely ball of worsted-weight yarn and the difficult inverted V-stitch. Very few people knew how to do the inverted V. But then, very few people were as passionate about crocheting as Ernest. There was nothing he loved more than looping and hooking, looping and hooking.

"No hobbies?" Mr. Jupiter asked again.

Ernest glanced at his new classmates. Would they be interested in crochet? He doubted it. They would probably think crocheting was as dull as vanilla ice cream. Sighing, he looked back at his shoes.

"Do you like poetry?" asked Lil.

Ernest shook his head.

"Do you like sports?" asked Jackie.

Ernest shook his head.

"Do you like *International Geographic* magazine?" asked Bruce.

Ernest shook his head.

He felt like a loser. A weirdo. A bobble-head doll.

"What *do* you like to do?" asked Missy.

Ernest swallowed hard. He had to say something. Anything. But what? Frantically, he scanned the room. A poster listing water facts caught his eye.

WATER, it read, IS GOOD FOR DRINKING, BATHING . . .

"Swimming," blurted Ernest. "I . . . I . . . swim!"

Swim? He couldn't believe his own ears. He couldn't swim. He couldn't even float. He opened his mouth to take it back, but—

"Do you swim just for fun?" asked Emberly.

"Or are you on a team?" asked Jackie.

Ernest looked around.

Amazing! His new classmates were looking at him with interest. They didn't think he was dull. They liked him!

Ernest puffed out his chest. "Back in Kathmandu I was captain of my swim team. I shot through the water like a silver arrow. I won ribbons, medals, gold cups. I—"

"That is fascinating," interrupted Mr. Jupiter. "But let's find you a place to sit."

"Here, here," squealed Bernadette.

"No, by me," hollered Lenny.

"I don't suppose he wants to sit by me," moaned Melvin.

Mr. Jupiter put Ernest in the empty desk between Humphrey and Amisha.

Then he clapped his hands again. "Class," he said, "please take out your copy of *Predicting, Inferring, Questioning, Visualizing, Determining Importance, and Making Connections Is Fun.*"

"What's that?" Ernest whispered to Amisha.

"Our reading book," she explained.

"Please turn to the vocabulary words on page eight hundred seventeen," Mr. Jupiter continued. "Who can give me the definition of *goblet*?"

Stanford raised his hand. "A small turkey."

"Precisely," said Mr. Jupiter. "Rose, can you tell me the meaning of the word *harvest*?"

"Something a farmer wears to cut down corn," answered Rose.

"Very good," said Mr. Jupiter.

In the back of the room, Humphrey moved his chair next to Ernest's. "Until you get a book, we can share," he said.

Ernest smiled. He was glad everyone seemed to like him. Or at least they liked Ernest the exciting champion swimmer. He wondered if they would like Ernest the boring crocheter.

Over the next few days, Ernest fell into the fourth-grade routine—music with Mr. Halfnote every Tuesday; gym with Mrs. Gluteal every Wednesday; library time with Miss Turner every Thursday.

"Who's that?" asked Ernest the first time he saw

Miss Turner. She was wearing a clingy green dress, tall green sandals, and dangly green earrings. Beneath the library's fluorescent light, her bright blond hair shimmered as she flitted from Fiction to Biography to Book Return.

Lenny looked up from the latest issue of *International Geographic*. "That's just the librarian."

"She doesn't look like a librarian," said Ernest.

"But she acts like one," said Bruce.

"Shhhh," said Miss Turner.

"See?" said Bruce.

Ernest adjusted to Mr. Jupiter, too.

"Are you really an honorary member of the Athabascan tribe of Alaska?" he asked his new teacher one day.

"I certainly am," replied Mr. Jupiter. He pointed to a corner of the classroom. "And there's the totem pole to prove it."

Ernest even grew comfortable with his new classmates. And when Ernest felt comfortable, he crocheted— book covers, desk doilies, backpacks.

"This is beautiful," said Missy, holding up a glue bottle cozy in a crisscross design. "Where'd you buy it?"

"Yeah, where?" asked Ham. "I want one."

"I'd rather have one of those seat covers," said Emberly.

"Not me," said Victoria. "I want one of those hanging scissors holders. Except I want mine in blue to match my eyes."

Ernest's heart leaped with joy. They liked his creations. Maybe if he told the truth, it would be okay. But before he could speak, Mr. Jupiter clapped his hands.

"Just a reminder," he said, "our field trip is tomorrow. Everyone should dress appropriately."

All the fourth graders except Emberly whooped.

He scratched his left arm, his right ear, and his tummy.

Ernest turned to Humphrey. "Field trip? What field trip? Where?"

"To the natatorium," said Humphrey.

"Huh?" asked Ernest.

"The swimming pool," translated Stanford.

"Sw . . . sw . . . swimming pool?" stammered Ernest.

"Aren't you thrilled?" asked Rose.

"Yeah," said Jackie, "we'll finally get to see you shoot through the water like a silver arrow."

Ernest pulled the collar of his hand-crocheted sweater over his head. "I'm doomed," he groaned.

The next morning, the fourth-grade classroom bulged with beach bags, foam footballs, inflatable rafts, kickboards, and nose plugs. Ernest shivered and pulled the bathrobe he had crocheted tighter around him.

"Oooh," said Victoria. "That's stunning. Where'd you get it?"

But before he could tell her, Mr. Jupiter said, "Quickly, class, let's take attendance. Is anyone absent?"

"Emberly is," said Ham.

"Too bad," said Mr. Jupiter. He wrote down Emberly's name, then said, "Anyone else?"

"Rachel," said Bernadette.

"Pffft," Rachel said. She snapped Bernadette with her beach towel.

"Oh, look," said Bernadette. "Rachel just walked in."

"Anyone else?" asked Mr. Jupiter.

"Nope," said Lenny.

"*Nada,*" said Bruce.

"Nary a one," said Lil, and she waxed poetic.

"We are all here,
With smiles, bag lunches,
And loads of good cheer."

"Then let's head for the bus," said Mr. Jupiter. His flip-flops snapped, and the Dipsy Duck swim ring around his waist squeaked as he led the way.

Ernest found a seat next to Humphrey.

"I can't wait to see you shoot through the water like a silver arrow," Humphrey said.

Ernest couldn't answer. His tongue was too thick with fear. Clutching his hand-crocheted towel like a security blanket, he slid down in his seat and prayed for an earthquake . . . an alien invasion . . . a flat tire.

But he had no such luck.

Minutes later, the bus dropped the kids off at the pool.

"Geronimo!" shrieked Bernadette, and she cannonballed into the water.

"Banzai!" cried Amisha, and she belly-flopped into the water.

"Watch this!" cried Melvin, and he did a reverse with a one-and-a-half somersault and three twists into the water.

The others ignored him.

On the edge of the pool, Ernest mustered all his courage and dipped his big toe just as Jackie raced up beside him. "C'mon, the water's fine." She slapped Ernest hard on the back.

Ernest teetered on the brink, then—

SPLASH!

He fell in.

Ernest thrashed, flapped, floundered. "Help!" he sputtered. "I can't swim!"

The others shot through the water like silver arrows. Heaving Ernest up and onto the side of the pool, they gathered around as he lay gasping for air.

Everyone could see the truth at a glance.

"I guess this means you don't swim," said Jackie.

"I guess," said Ernest when he was finally able to speak.

"What a big fake," muttered the others.

"Pffft," scolded Rachel.

Then Missy said, "Tell the truth. Is there anything you like to do?"

Ernest took a deep breath. "I . . . I . . . crochet."

"Crochet?" repeated Humphrey.

Ernest nodded.

"As in bathrobes and book covers and glue bottle cozies?" asked Victoria.

Ernest nodded.

"Can you teach us?" begged Calvin. "I want one of those vests, too."

Ernest nodded.

Yes, he felt like a bobble-head doll.

But he felt like a winner, too.

MORAL: Those who pretend to be what they are not, sooner or later find themselves in deep water.

HUMPHREY'S LUNCH

EVERY SPRING DURING NATIONAL
Nutrition Week, Mrs. Gluteal gave a lecture on healthy eating.

This year was no exception.

"Gather around," said Mrs. Gluteal when Mr. Jupiter's class stepped into the gymnasium. She pointed to a gigantic food pyramid taped to the wrestling mat.

"Not again," moaned Humphrey Parrot. Then, in perfect imitation of the gym teacher, he said, " 'Food is the fuel that runs our engines.' "

Rose giggled.

" 'You are what you eat,' " Humphrey continued.

Lenny laughed.

" 'Food,' " added Humphrey, " 'it does a body good.' "

"Humphrey," said Mr. Jupiter, "sit down, please."

Humphrey joined the rest of the class on the polished wood floor. He had a perfect view of Mrs. Gluteal's hair-stubbled knees.

"Food," began Mrs. Gluteal, "is the fuel that runs our engines."

Humphrey's eyes glazed over. His stomach growled, and his thoughts strayed to lunch.

He had packed it himself.

"Can you make your lunch just this once?" his mom had asked that morning. "I've got an early meeting, and I'm already running late. "

"Sure, Mom," he had replied.

"And don't forget the carrot sticks," she'd called as she hurried out the door.

Humphrey detested carrots.

Now Mr. Jupiter tapped him on the shoulder, and Humphrey suddenly found himself back in the gymnasium.

"You are what you eat," Mrs. Gluteal was saying.

Mr. Jupiter leaned close. "Are you paying attention, Humphrey?" he whispered.

Humphrey shrugged. "I know all about good eating," he whispered back. "This is the third time I've heard this lecture."

"You know what they say in Bora-Bora," replied Mr. Jupiter. "*Tapiti maita vau,* or 'Three times is a charm.' "

Humphrey's stomach growled again.

"So in conclusion," said Mrs. Gluteal, "food. It does a body good."

The bell rang.

"Lunchtime!" whooped Humphrey.

At the long lunchroom table, Humphrey elbowed between Calvin and Emberly. Eagerly, he opened his Eleanor Roosevelt lunch box. Out came a can of orange soda, a package of salty chips, a chocolate cupcake, and a bacon sandwich on white bread slathered in mayonnaise.

He lifted the sandwich to his lips.

"Poison!"

Startled, Humphrey looked up to find Mrs. Gluteal standing in front of him. "Humphrey Parrot," she lectured. "Just look at this unhealthy mess—sugar, salt, fat! It's all so bad for you!"

Like a buzzard, she swooped down and swept up his lunch. Only a lonely dollop of mayonnaise remained in front of him.

"But . . . but . . . I'm hungry!" wailed Humphrey.

"Of course you are," said Mrs. Gluteal. "You're hungry for something healthy. You're hungry for real nourishment. You're hungry for good nutrition. Therefore, Humphrey, I am going to make the supreme sacrifice. I am going to give you *my* lunch."

She dropped a spinach salad topped with tofu and goat cheese in front of him.

"Enjoy," she said, and she turned and walked away.

Humphrey's friends gazed at the salad.

"Gross," said Emberly. He took a happy bite of his own tuna pita.

"Super gross," said Calvin. He merrily crunched on one of his cucumber slices.

"Super-duper gross," said Ham. He joyfully slurped up some of the cook's newest specialty—yak and cheese.

Humphrey's stomach growled again.

Cautiously, he speared a tiny piece of tofu with his plastic fork. He nibbled.

"Not bad," he said.

He took another, bigger bite.

"Not bad at all."

He took several bites in a row.

"Strangely satisfying," he declared.

He gobbled up the salad.

The bell rang.

"Recess!" hollered Humphrey. The salad had left him feeling unusually energized. "Who wants to play tetherball?"

"ME!" cried Emberly and Calvin in unison.

The boys headed for the blacktop.

But as they passed the teachers' lounge, the door suddenly burst open and Miss Turner, led by Miss Fairchild, stepped out. Miss Turner had her eyes squeezed shut.

"Really, Paige," Miss Fairchild was saying, "those fake eyelashes are lovely, but they're bound to fall off if you flutter them so much."

Through the open door, Humphrey spied Mrs. Gluteal. Mayonnaise dripped down her chin as she brushed chocolate crumbs from her mouth with bacon-greasy fingers. "Does anyone want a salty chip?" Humphrey heard her say before the door slammed shut. "They're delicious."

For a moment Humphrey stared at the door of the teachers' lounge. Then he shrugged. "I guess Mrs. Gluteal hasn't been listening to her own lecture. If she had been, she'd know—"

"You are what you eat!" cried Emberly and Calvin in unison.

High-fiving each other, the boys raced off to recess.

MORAL: Practice what you preach.

THE SPELLING GODDESS

MR. JUPITER'S STUDENTS WERE TAKING their weekly spelling test.

"The first word," said Mr. Jupiter, "is *nincompoop*. *Nincompoop* sounds like a naughty made-up word, but it is actually in the dictionary. *Nincompoop*."

Ashlee A. moved her lips, trying to sound out the word.

Ashleigh B. shut her eyes, trying to see the word in her mind.

Ashley Z. stretched his neck, trying to see the word on Stanford's paper.

"Ashley," said Mr. Jupiter, "I hope I didn't see you looking at your neighbor's work."

"I hope you didn't either," replied Ashley.

At her desk, Amisha Spelwadi wrote the word with quick, sure strokes. "Easy-peasy," she said under her breath. She covered her answer with her arm.

"The second word," said Mr. Jupiter, "is *wildebeest*. While hiking across the Serengeti, I was once attacked by a wildebeest. *Wildebeest*."

Calvin chewed nervously on his pencil eraser.

Rachel frowned, wrote, and erased, frowned, wrote, and erased.

But Amisha didn't hesitate. "Easier-peasier," she said in a voice a bit louder. She wrote the word down, then held her head high. She wanted the rest of her classmates to know *she* wasn't having any spelling trouble. She smiled smugly at Mr. Jupiter.

"The third word," said Mr. Jupiter, "is *gaseous*. If you eat the cook's hot lunch, you are bound to become gaseous. *Gaseous*."

Jackie looked frantically around the room, hoping to see the word written on the chalkboard, a poster, a book spine, anywhere!

Rose gave a little sob.

But Amisha quickly scrawled the word on her paper. "Easiest-peasiest," she said in a very loud voice.

Victoria shot her a dirty look.

But Amisha didn't care. She was floating! Soaring! She was a spelling goddess!

She breezed through the rest of the words too.

Foofaraw.

Booby hatch.

Pogonip.

Cat.

Amisha was sure she knew them all.

I'm going to get the whole test right, she told herself. She began turning over in her mind what would happen when she received a perfect test score. *My classmates will cheer, and Mr. Jupiter will declare me the best speller in the fourth grade. I'll go on to win the school spelling bee, then the state spelling bee, then the national spelling bee! I'll become such a famous speller that my face will be on the cover of magazines . . . newspapers . . . cereal boxes! I'll be on talk shows and in commercials and I'll become so famous that everyone will want to be just like me. Of course, Hollywood will make a movie of my life. With all my movie money, I'll build a big castle, and I'll have lots of puppies, and horses, and fancy butlers who'll serve me chocolate milk shakes in crystal goblets. And I'll travel around and around the world meeting kings and queens and princes. They'll be so awed by my spelling skills they'll make me an honorary princess. From then on, everyone will call me Princess Amisha. And I'll wear a diamond tiara every day—even to school—and Victoria Sovaine will turn pea green with envy. And I'll buy my friends diamond tiaras too, and Victoria will cry and wish she'd been nicer to me, but I won't buy her anything. And then I'll take—*

Mr. Jupiter clapped his hands. "Please exchange your test papers with the person behind you," he said.

Eagerly, Amisha handed her paper to Melvin, then accepted Lil's.

Ooooh! She could hardly wait until the spelling tests had been checked.

Oooh! Oooh! She could hardly wait until everyone saw her perfect score.

Minutes later, Melvin handed back her paper.

No!

It couldn't be!

But it was.

She had spelled *cat* with . . . a *k*.

With a sigh, Amisha opened her spelling book and began working on next week's words.

Slubbering.

Podunk.

Tittle-tattle.

Dog.

MORAL: Don't count your chickens before they're hatched.

FIRST KISS

IN JUNE THE FOURTH GRADERS FOUND Miss Turner sobbing behind Love and Customs (Dewey decimal number 392).

"What's the matter?" asked Missy. "Did you lose your mittens?"

"Did you catch the chicken pox?" asked Emberly.

"Did Melvil Dewey die?" asked Lenny.

"No, no," sniffled Miss Turner. "It's nothing like that."

"Then what's the problem?" asked Mr. Jupiter.

Miss Turner turned to him, her eyes shining with tears . . . and something more. "Don't you know?" she asked in a voice throbbing with emotion. "Haven't you guessed?"

"I can guess," Ernest said.

"Me too," Ham said, "and I'm only in fourth grade."

Mr. Jupiter shot the boys a warning look. Then he said, "Children, go read a book, please."

"Read a book?" said Amisha.

"And miss all the excitement?" said Lil.

Mr. Jupiter's face turned stony. "Go!"

The children went—but only as far as Espionage and Spying (Dewey decimal number 327). They peeked around the bookshelf.

Mr. Jupiter turned his attention back to the librarian. "I have no idea what you're talking about, Paige."

Miss Turner burst into a fresh round of tears. "That's exactly the problem," she wailed. "You have no idea."

Mr. Jupiter looked confused. "I still don't understand."

Bernadette looked at Victoria. "For a teacher, he's not too smart," she whispered.

"She's going to have to explain it to him," Victoria whispered back.

"Let me explain it to you," sniffled Miss Turner.

"Told you so," whispered Victoria.

Swallowing her tears, Miss Turner said, "All year I've tried to get your attention. I've bought new clothes. I've dyed my hair. I've even tortured myself with these teetering, too-tight shoes. But have you noticed? No! To you, I'm still that mousy librarian you met during your first week at Aesop Elementary."

Mr. Jupiter looked even more confused. "Mousy?"

he repeated. He shook his head. "I didn't see a mousy librarian that first day. I saw an interesting woman."

"You did?" said Miss Turner. She blew her nose wetly.

Mr. Jupiter nodded. "Your wire-rimmed glasses reflected your intelligence, and your cardigan—the one with the apples appliquéd on it, if I remember correctly—matched your personality."

"It did?" said Miss Turner. She dried her mascara-rimmed eyes.

Mr. Jupiter nodded again. "Honestly, Paige. I liked you just the way you were."

"You did?" said Miss Turner.

"I did," said Mr. Jupiter.

They gazed at each other.

"Barf-o-rama," shuddered Ham. "I think they're going to kiss."

"I can't watch," groaned Jackie. She covered her eyes.

"Quick!" cried Humphrey. "Somebody warn Mr. Jupiter about cooties."

But it was too late.

Mr. Jupiter leaned down and touched his lips to the librarian's cheek.

"Awww," cooed the girls.

"Blecch," gagged the boys.

"I'll never wash this cheek again," said Miss Turner. "And tomorrow? I'm wearing my cardigan."

MORAL: Appearances aren't everything.

MR. JUPITER TAKES
THE FIFTH

ON THE LAST DAY OF SCHOOL, MR.
Jupiter's students cleaned out their desks. They tossed
out pencil nubs, gum wrappers, half-empty glue bot-
tles, and tests with bad grades.

"Oh, look!" Missy suddenly shouted. "I found my
mittens." She pulled out thirty-six pairs of black knitted mittens.

"Oh, gross," moaned Rose. "I found that first class
picture."

"Oh, joy!" cried Ham. "I found a green jelly bean."

He popped it into his mouth just as Humphrey said,
"That's not a jelly bean. That's a moldy piece of tofu
from one of my salads."

Ham smacked his lips. "It was still good."

"I bet you're going to be sick," said Emberly. "I bet
you're going to puke the whole first week of summer
vacation and not be able to go to the swimming pool."

"That's okay," said Ernest. "He can always stay
home and crochet with me."

"Pffft," said Rachel.

Nobody heard her.

"Yikes," said Jackie. "I hope I don't catch it. I catch everything, you know—baseballs, basketballs, Frisbees."

"Get serious," snorted Stanford. "You can't catch food poisoning."

Mr. Jupiter clapped his hands. "It's time to collect the textbooks. Please pass your spelling manuals to the front."

Amisha handed hers forward. "Goodbye, old friend," she whispered.

"Now your math books," Mr. Jupiter said a few moments later.

Calvin handed his forward. "Goodbye and good riddance," he whispered.

"And now your organic geochemistry books," Mr. Jupiter finally said.

"Hey," cried Melvin, "I never got one of those!"

The others ignored him.

"Is everyone's desk finally empty?" asked Mr. Jupiter.

"Mine is," said Lil. And she waxed poetic:

"O empty desk,
Once full of books,
Now full of air,
You sit,
Forlornly,
Waiting for next year."

The sadness of her poem touched the other students.

Gloomily, they looked around at the classroom's bare walls and empty shelves. Mr. Jupiter had already taken home his collections of meteorites and Mexican jumping beans. He'd packed up his Tibetan prayer wheel and his Mongolian camel saddle. He'd even hauled away his army-ant farm and his anaconda skin. Now the place was merely a shell of its former self.

"I feel sort of sad," said Calvin.

"Me too," said Bernadette.

"Now, now," said Mr. Jupiter. "It may be the last day of school, but it's the first day of summer. Who has exciting plans?"

Ham's eyes sparkled with happiness. "I'm spending two weeks with my grandparents in Hershey, Pennsylvania."

"I'm going to modeling camp," said Victoria.

"I'm getting my own subscription to *International Geographic*," said Lenny.

"What are you doing, Mr. Jupiter?" Ashlee B. asked.

"I will be embarking on the greatest adventure of my life," he replied.

"What's that?" asked Jackie. "Touring America's baseball parks?"

"No," said Mr. Jupiter. "I'm going to Mars."

"Mars!" the children gasped.

Mr. Jupiter nodded. "I've been invited by the International Space Academy to help establish a colony there. I'm hoping to open the first interplanetary elementary school in history."

"Wow," said Ashley Z. "That's a lot for one summer."

"Actually," said Mr. Jupiter, "I'll be on Mars for years." He paused, then added, "Today is my last day at Aesop Elementary School."

"No!" cried Missy.

"It can't be true!" wailed Emberly.

"Now I feel really sad," sobbed Calvin.

Stanford raised his hand. "Who's going to be our teacher next year?" he asked.

Everyone knew that Mr. Lipschitz, the fifth-grade teacher, had decided to retire early rather than teach the upcoming class.

"Yes, who?" repeated Humphrey.

"I don't know," said Mr. Jupiter. "But I'm sure your new teacher will be a caring, loving person who will recognize each and every one of your unique qualities."

At that moment, Miss Turner breezed into the classroom.

"Why so gloomy?" she asked when she saw the children's faces.

"Mr. Jupiter's leaving us!" blurted Rose. "He's going to Mars."

The color drained from Miss Turner's cheeks. "But who will teach the children?" she asked.

The classroom door burst open, and in stalked a man dressed entirely in black and carrying a mysterious leather satchel. He glowered at the children from beneath bushy gray eyebrows.

And Mr. Jupiter turned as white as his whale tooth necklace. He ducked behind Miss Turner.

"What are you doing?" she shrieked.

"Shhh," whispered Mr. Jupiter.

Miss Turner lowered her voice. "What's going on?"

"I've stood at the edge of an erupting volcano," Mr. Jupiter whispered frantically, "swum through shark-infested waters, survived an attack of killer bees. But there's still one thing that strikes fear into my heart—"

"My name is Hermann Kinderschmacker," growled the man.

"And he's it," squeaked Mr. Jupiter. He stuck his head under Miss Turner's cardigan.

"I will be your fifth-grade teacher," Mr. Kinderschmacker continued. He smiled menacingly. "And I have ways of making you behave."

Rose gulped.

Rachel gasped.

And Mr. Jupiter whimpered.

The sound made Mr. Kinderschmacker turn. "Who's there?" he demanded. "Come out at once."

On legs that were weaker than Calvin's math skills, Mr. Jupiter stepped out from behind the librarian. "H . . . h . . . hi there, Mr. K . . . K . . . Kinderschmacker." He tried to sound nonchalant.

"Well, well, if it isn't my old student, Harry Valentine Jupiter," growled Mr. Kinderschmacker.

Mr. Jupiter tried to smile.

"Where's your homework?" snapped the fifth-grade teacher.

"H . . . h . . . homework?" squeaked Mr. Jupiter. "It's been twenty-five years since I've been in your class. I don't remember any h . . . h . . . homework."

"I do," snarled Mr. Kinderschmacker. "You never turned in your final math assignment. We were studying decimals." He took a step toward his former pupil. "What do you have to say for yourself, Harry Valentine?"

Mr. Jupiter searched his mind for an excuse, *any* excuse. "W . . . w . . . would you believe I lost it fighting this k . . . k . . . kid who said you weren't the b . . . b . . . best teacher in the school?" he stammered.

"Hey, that's *my* excuse," said Lenny.

But Mr. Kinderschmacker sneered. "I never believe ANYTHING my students tell me. You know that." And he snapped open his satchel and pulled out a fifth-grade math book.

At the sight of it, Calvin almost fainted.

"You will do page fifty-eight—now!" thundered Mr. Kinderschmacker.

"But . . . but . . . ," began Mr. Jupiter.

"No buts," warned Mr. Kinderschmacker, "or *else*."

Mr. Jupiter yelped, grabbed the book, and sat down at his desk. As he struggled with the first two hundred and fifty-seven math problems, Mr. Kinderschmacker turned back to the students.

"In my classroom you will work," he barked. "Not only will you be expected to copy each of your spelling words five hundred times a week, but you will be required to turn in one hundred book reports a month, AND do six hours of homework each night." He looked around the room. "Any questions?"

"Will we tell jokes?" asked Lenny.

"Absolutely not!"

"Will we get snacks?" asked Ham.

"Never!"

"Will we be given time to crochet?" asked Ernest.

"Don't make me laugh!"

Missy turned to Rose. "I didn't think he *could* laugh," she whispered.

"Stop that jibber-jabber at once!" roared Mr. Kinderschmacker.

"Hey," said Humphrey. "You can't talk to us like that."

"I certainly can," replied Mr. Kinderschmacker. "I'm the teacher. Now, everyone shut your mouths and lay your heads on your desks. You will remain that way until the end of the day."

Meekly, the children put their heads down.

"But Mr. Kinderschmacker," said Miss Turner, "may I remind you that there are still four more hours of school?"

"Silence!" shouted the new teacher. "Do as I said."

Meekly, the librarian put her head down too.

Soon the room grew quiet. Only the sound of Calvin nervously chewing on his pencil broke the silence.

Then Rachel began whimpering so loudly that the others could almost hear her.

Stanford began blithering like an idiot.

Victoria began miserably picking at her new French manicure.

Lil began mumbling a dirge.

And Ham complained about loss of appetite.

All this noise forced Mr. Jupiter to look up from his decimals. What he saw shocked him.

Lenny and Bruce were clinging to each other, and they looked . . . terrified!

"NOOOOO!" screamed Mr. Jupiter. Leaping to his feet, he swept the math book onto the floor. It landed with an explosive BAM!

"That's a month's detention for you, Harry Valentine," snarled Mr. Kinderschmacker.

Mr. Jupiter suddenly felt courage coursing through his veins. It reminded him of the time he had wrestled a crocodile on the banks of the Nile River. He lifted his chin. "No," he said. "It's not."

"Sit down," commanded Mr. Kinderschmacker.

Mr. Jupiter squared his shoulders. "No," he said. "I won't."

"This is my class now," hissed Mr. Kinderschmacker.

Mr. Jupiter stood tall. "No," he said. "This is *my* class, and these are *my* students."

The children raised their heads. "But what about exploring Mars?" they asked.

"And establishing an interplanetary school?" added Miss Turner.

"Colonization of Mars can wait," Mr. Jupiter replied, "but my students can't."

Mr. Kinderschmacker growled. "I intend to speak to the principal about this."

"It won't do any good," said Mr. Jupiter. "She likes me better."

Mr. Kinderschmacker growled again. "You were

always a troublemaker." Stuffing the math book back into his satchel, he strode toward the door. But before crossing the threshold, he turned. "I'll be back, Harry Valentine. Mark my words. I'll be back."

Then he was gone. All the almost fifth graders clapped, cheered, and leaped from their seats, surrounding their teacher.

Bruce was so happy, he hugged Mr. Jupiter.

Jackie was so happy, *she* hugged Mr. Jupiter.

Stanford was so happy, he shook Mr. Jupiter's hand.

Then everyone took turns hugging Mr. Jupiter or shaking his hand.

Everyone, that is, except Miss Turner. She took the opportunity to plant a kiss on Mr. Jupiter's cheek. "You're a good man, Harry Valentine," she said.

Mr. Jupiter blushed.

And Lenny suddenly whooped, "Fifth grade, here we come!"

"Yes indeed," said Mr. Jupiter. "And it's bound to be an adventure."

MORAL: There is a time and place for everything.